Jurassichrist

Michael Allen Rose

PMMP

Perpetual Motion Machine Publishing
Cibolo, Texas

Jurassichrist
Copyright © 2021 Michael Allen Rose

All Rights Reserved

ISBN: 978-1-943720-57-6

www.PerpetualPublishing.com

Cover Art by Lori Michelle

For Sauda, who always believes.
And for all the nonbelievers.

Genesis

It wasn't supposed to be like this. J.C. cut a swath through the jungle, tearing long drooping tropical leaves from their branches with the lightning swing of his machete. Around him, the lush jungle foliage drizzled down droplets of moisture, covering the jungle floor in a stew of mud, plant matter, and animal droppings. The ground sucked at his right sandal, and he pulled it loose with a distinct pop before re-adjusting it on his filthy foot. What he wouldn't give for a nice set of combat boots right about now.

He checked his ammunition, tightening his ammo belt and counting by reflex. Fingering the grenades attached to his utility belt, he paused. The sweat dripping down his forehead was stinging his eyes, and the headband tied snugly around his cranium did little to alleviate his suffering.

He would fight on. He'd suffered much worse than this.

The emerald canopy above him shuddered for a moment, and J.C. went into a crouch, pointing the barrel of his massive machine gun upward at an angle. The treetops shifted with the breeze, high above the ground. Had it merely been a change in the direction of the wind? Or was there something moving up there? The feeling of being hunted had been a constant spear in his side since he'd entered this section of the jungle. His pursuers were far behind him, weren't they? His bright brown eyes scanned the foliage above. If there were eyes in the air, he needed to knock them out of commission before the commotion attracted undue attention.

J.C. unwound a section of his tripwire roll and secured it to a flexible stick lying nearby. He knotted it in the appropriate way, so that it would slide. He then carefully tied it to the rope from his combat pack and, dragging the other end across the mud, quietly moved into cover. His robes allowed him to slip into a large group of ferns relatively unencumbered. As he peered from the bushes, his pupils dilated and he waited, focused like a laser on the small circle he'd made. With one quick motion, he reached down to his side, where his old wound still gaped, pinched a piece of his own flesh, tore it off and tossed it, wincing only a little. It landed dead center in the circle. Almost immediately, his flesh knit itself back together into a nasty, ragged scar, just above his kidneys. He knew that it would always heal, but never truly be right. In situations like this, it was useful to have a body that would re-generate, at least to a certain degree.

The small piece of meat glistened. J.C. focused his attention on his target, but he couldn't afford to ignore his surroundings. He had to maintain his tension and absorb everything going on around him, otherwise he could be easily overwhelmed with a surprise attack. He didn't want to test the limits of his regenerative powers between the jaws of some monster, as it crushed him between rows of its dagger-like teeth.

It only took a few moments before there was a crack from above, and a few small twigs fell from the canopy. Giant leathery wings stretched out as the creature burst through the treetops,

Michael Allen Rose

carrying with it a shadow that swallowed what little sunlight made it through to the ground, and granted the clearing a twilight condition.

Screeching, the monstrous thing dove down and opened its talons. With pinpoint precision, the flying creature snatched the piece of meat, but its talons raked the ground just enough for the supernatural reflexes of J.C. to spy his opportunity. He pulled the rope quickly, causing the loop to close and ensnare the creature's right foot.

"I have bound thee! Thou shalt not hunt me, for I am the predator, and thou art the prey!" J.C. leapt from the fern he had been perched in and grinned at his prize, but without hesitation, the creature continued its flight path and took off into the air once more. "Oh, no."

The immense wings flapped and J.C. felt like he was holding onto a tornado. He felt his feet being dragged through the sticky mud, and his shoulder muscles and arms strained trying to keep the creature from taking off. With a squawk of protest, the flying thing turned its pointy head and glared at J.C with beady, mean little eyes. Now, at the end of the rope, it flew in a wobbly circle around J.C. as he desperately tried to wrangle the monster's weight and power.

Jurassichrist

"Thou shalt not!" cried J.C. as he flexed his biceps and pulled his arms into his chest, throwing his weight opposite the monster's flight path, but it did little good, as he felt his sandal catch a rock embedded in the soft ground. J.C. stumbled, losing his sandal somewhere in the filthy muck and fell to his knees awkwardly. The rope slipped through his hands, as he desperately tried to get a grip. Rope burns flared up on either side of the holes through his palms, and he instinctively let go, cursing bitterly. (If he had been ready for things to go awry, and felt particularly reflexive, he might have gained the advantage by tying a bowline knot through one of his palms. However, the last time he'd done that, he'd ended up starting a small robe fire due to the friction, so he was less than enthusiastic about repeating that scenario.)

With a triumphant caw, the leathery flyer soared upward, trailing J.C.'s rope behind it like a mocking tail. J.C. could do nothing but watch, as the creature blasted through the treetops, parting the canopy above, and disappeared into the sky with his only rope.

The gun clicked into position and fired rounds into the sky, as J.C. waved the massive weapon back and forth, screaming. Flocks of tiny lizard-like things exploded skyward, trying to avoid being struck down by a wave of hot metal shards. His temper was usually easy to keep under control. He had been a man of peace, once. Now, he hated the idea that his name might be synonymous with war and destruction, but his boiling point had been reached. He jerked his finger from the trigger and let the gun drop to his side, feeling tears of frustration run down his cheeks. This didn't feel right. None of this felt right.

He looked down and sadly realized that his sandal was likely to go unrecovered. It had sunk into the foulness somewhere nearby, and the time it would take to find and retrieve it wasn't a luxury he could afford. Lopsided, with one sandal, rope burns, and an itchy wound knitting itself together at his side, J.C. sighed and muttered to himself. He couldn't lose focus now, despite this setback. He still had his guns, his ammo, and a large portion of his equipment. Most of all, he had his resolve to find someone capable of helping him get back home and fix this situation before things got worse on a cosmic scale.

No, it definitely was not supposed to be like this. That much was certain.

Book 1

It **was supposed** to be a simple matter of coming back to the place he'd already been. It was a second coming, an arrival that had long been foretold and planned for. Easy stuff. Child's play.

The universe had been built like celestial clockwork, a series of gears, wheels, and levers that all clicked together. Tones that resonated in perfect harmonious frequency. Nothing had been left to chance.

According to the architects and builders of this reality, there was no possibility of anything going awry. Therefore, J.C. hadn't worried too much about his task, monumental as it might have been, in theory. Besides that, he was the only being who'd transcended the planes in that direction and come back to tell about it. If anyone could handle it, surely the son of man himself could make short work of any obstacle he came up against.

Admittedly, there had been a few glitches the first time around.

He made friends, and that had been nice. Fishing buddies, people to listen to his speeches, the whole deal. Even though a couple of them had turned out to be dicks in the end, with betrayals and denials. But, that had been accounted for. It was all part of the "transcending this mortal coil" situation.

Of course, he didn't completely realize what that whole "dying to get back home" plan would entail. Nobody mentioned that he might get stabbed in the liver by a drunk Roman soldier. Sure, the military man had ostensibly done so to help speed up his death and eliminate unnecessary suffering, but had no way to know that J.C.'s healing factor would basically just make it more agonizing. Also, the holes in his extremities were incredibly inconvenient. Anything he tried to hold in the palm of his hand, like say if he was counting grains of sand or measuring out chili powder for his hot chocolate, fell right through.

Jurassichrist

The boards they strapped him to were full of splinters, and the contraption was heavy, as he knew, since they made him carry the damned thing all the way up the hill. The whole situation was kind of a shit-show, as far as he was concerned.

But, J.C. was a tough bastard, and he knew his duty. When he'd been tasked with this crazy plan, and told that cosmic balance was at stake, he had stepped up and done what was necessary. Really, in the end, it turned out pretty okay. It took a few days to get through all the red tape, and fuel his superself with enough energy to transcend the mortal frame he'd been inhabiting and fly off, but once he ascended and blew the minds of the puny mortals around him, he was in the clear. When he got back home, the whole place was decked out for a party, and the celebration was epic indeed.

Celestials flying all over the place, having airborne races drunk to the gills on manna wine. Random collections of animal parts brought to life and paraded around to do tricks for the amusement of the audience. All the seraphim were shooting pure, uncut stardust from every orifice, leading the whole cloudy city of the celestials to feel the magical tingle of intoxication.

Michael Allen Rose

J.C. was a hero. Parades. Autographs. They even inflated some gas planets and let them float around the sky in colorful bunches. The celebration lasted for an amount of time that was best described as just next to infinity. It could have gone on (literally) forever, but again, his sense of duty had come into play, and the second coming, long prophesied about, was overdue.

The second coming was going to be new and improved. Even greater than the first. A slick new package that spoke to the contemporary mores and foibles of human society, and really rocked some faces off. It was to be the heavy metal liquid explosion of the theological, a true universally felt quake in the fabric of time and space. Since the first trip had been relatively successful, J.C. figured that this would be cake. He had charisma, experience, a fighting spirit, and a plan.

What could possibly go wrong?

His relationship to the time-space continuum, for starters. Unfortunately, it turns out, linear time progression doesn't apply to extra-spatial deities.

Your typical mortal creature views time as a linear process that is immutable. They just sort of drift along through time like a toy boat in a stream, crashing into the occasional rock and trying not to get too soggy on their inevitable journey toward death and the entropy of sinking. Mortals don't have the capacity to understand and perceive time in any other way, with their puny, limited senses. (Most children would list five senses, with some neurologists listing as many as nine or even up to twenty-one. The sense that allows celestial beings to perceive time as a cloudy three-dimensional bubble is called "fnorkblart," and if they were aware of it, human beings would list it as the three-hundred and forty-seventh sense.)

Perhaps it was the literal "angel dust" that clouded their fnorkblart, or maybe it was just one great big cosmic mistake, but the engineers who had pushed the cosmic button to make the magic work had been off the mark.

" . . . on the cosmo-lunatic scale, it would be period seventeen point three seven six . . . "

" . . . that's not right, we're working on an anthrocentric calendar system . . . "

" . . . well, what's the conversion rate from chrono units to annuals?"

" . . . depends on the geography. Remember, we're working with a limited palate of dimensions here, so we have to divide the units into . . ."

" . . . why can't he just go back as a ghost, then we don't have to worry about the physical stress of matter generation?"

All these conversations had taken place around him, but J.C. hadn't given them a second thought. His instincts were pure. He would hone in on the humans himself. After all, he'd actually been one. What did the eggheads know, with their theoretical understanding of mortality and chronospatial existence? J.C. had fucking *died*. He had experienced both a beginning and an end. He understood time better than anyone here. He had practice.

Alas, thirty-three years as a human wasn't really that much experience, when you think about it. Most humans live somewhere between eighty and a hundred years, unless something goes wrong, and even the oldest of them couldn't begin to explain how time works. Hell, the ancient Sumerians pretty much invented the hour, the minute, and the second, and not one of them could tell you how time relates to the electronic transmission of the cesium atom.

The reality J.C.'s "dad" had set up was stuck following the second law of thermodynamics,

which states that within a closed system, the
entropy of the system remains constant or
increases. This is called time's arrow. If the
universe is considered to be a closed system, its
entropy, or degree of disorder, can never
decrease. In other words, the universe cannot
return to exactly the same state in which it was
at an earlier point. The arrow always shoots
forward.

Of course anyone worth their fnorkblart
knows that time is a bubble.

Ever shoot a bubble with an arrow?

For J.C. and his infinite, omnipresent self,
the second coming was like firing a bullet at a
target and trying to hit the hair stuck to it
without actually hitting anything else, including
the target itself.

As J.C. blasted through the cosmos at
299,792,459 metres per second, exactly 1 mps
faster than the speed of light, he took stock of
himself and his situation. As he checked
himself out, he realized that something was
amiss. A call to dad would be the best way to
lodge a complaint.

Seven trumpets later, YHWH finally picked
up.

"Hello?" His voice, usually booming like

thunder, was weirdly quiet and enmeshed in static.

"Dad? Is that thou?"

. . . bzzt crackle . . . "What is it, J.C.? Aren't you supposed to be on your second coming?"

J.C. tapped the side of his skull. "Dad, the reception is terrible. Art thou busy?"

"Yes. What's wrong?"

J.C. looked through the center of his right hand. There was a neat circle punched out of the middle, and he could see the swirling cosmos through it. The effect was a bit nauseating, a feeling that he hadn't missed outside of his mortal body—a grim reminder that he was not at home anymore.

"Dad, this is the same body I had last time. Did thou make any repairs at all?"

Silence, on the other end of the line. Then, after a moment: "I wanted you to be comfortable. Nobody wants you to waste precious time learning how to be human again."

"It's not that hard, Dad! Thou shalt ought have given me an upgrade. The mortals wouldst more likely listen to me if I were to be a total hottie. Thou ought to have made me a ten, where I feel that I have been given the body of a seven, in the best light."

Jurassichrist

"What was that?" **crackle** "You're breaking up. Hey, good luck down there, and don't forget, whatever you do, just—"

Static overtook the signal, leaving only the sounds remaining from the Big Bang to resonate through J.C.'s skull. Even without this distraction, it would have been almost impossible to adjust his trajectory through time and space, for he was close to the point of no return when he thought he saw a gleaming blue light. Was it a mark of civilization?

J.C. turned his newly reformed physical shell toward the light, peering through the void, trying to fixate on the illuminated point. "That has to be the nuclear age. Mid-twentieth century. Cool. Almost there." J.C. pulled his tinted goggles down from his forehead, across the halo of thorn marks, and secured them over his eyes. He gritted his teeth and twisted his body into what he thought would be an impressive pose. He had limited summoning capabilities, and could work minor creation miracles, but given the circumstances, he thought it would make the most impact if he landed as himself, the original, one-and-only J.C. There would be plenty of time to study the locals and conjure up the right look to blend in

~15~

with whatever society had become over the last two millennia.

Thus, due to all of the factors discussed herein, including a general lack of understanding about how limiting the confines of space and time really are, and the inability to correctly calculate for all four dimensions (X, Y, Z, and of course, the surprisingly confusing unidirectional time flow for mortals) did J.C. himself, son of god and king of kings, find himself spinning wildly toward the ground in a very hot and humid climate, careening toward what he was pretty sure should have been Earth's 21st century in the Middle East, about to come again. But he was not in the Middle East at all. Nor was he in the 21st century. The continent he smacked into was actually a great deal larger than what would come to be known as Eurasia.

One immense sonic boom later, and a weird phasing of the curtain of reality, and there he was, back on good old Earth, ready to lead the human race to a new and better existence.

He had managed to land upright, in what he considered a heroic sort of pose. It was the kind of thing expected of a magical celebrity from the sky. Slowly, breathing heavily in the damp atmosphere of Pangaea, he looked around, extending his jazz hands and smiling. There were no onlookers. No crowds. Nobody to impress. Given the infestation of Mother Earth by the human race, the statistical likelihood of him landing in some sort of population center was high, especially because they had carefully calibrated everything to miss the ocean. But, there was nothing here.

J.C. frowned and stood up. His robes were filthy, covered in sticky mud from where he had landed. There were no signs of civilization. But he'd seen that massive light, and it certainly wasn't natural—nothing he or his kind had put there—so where the hell were the people?

"Michael. Come in, Michael. We have a situation." J.C. knew that his pal back home would have some answers for him, but for some reason, his hailing went unanswered.

It wasn't even physical equipment. How could it be malfunctioning? For a being that existed outside of time and space, it was very confusing to not simply be able to reach through the veil and see, talk to, go toward or otherwise interact with anything, anywhere, at any point in the four most basic dimensions. Could it be that some accident had occurred?

Or worse yet, could someone have sabotaged the mission? Surely, that was impossible. Still, J.C. remembered his old pal Lucifer, and how poor Lucy had been thrown out on his ass for bringing the humans knowledge. That's why his nickname had always been "light-bearer." That, and his habit for lighting manna on fire before snorting it at parties.

So there was precedent for things going awry. Wrenches thrown into the cosmic gears. But, try as he might, J.C. couldn't think of anybody in the multiverse who would want this mission to fail. The whole point of the plan was to bring humanity up into the ranks of the celestials, a project everyone was invested in. The research and development budget for project humanity alone had been staggering in its scope, so even the most curmudgeonly of extra-dimensional beings wanted his second coming to hit the mark.

He tried to find any clues as to his whereabouts.

Steaming, hot mud pits. A lush jungle filled with flowering plants. Somewhere in the distance, he heard a sort of cross between a roar and a cackling screech.

"What the . . . " Something crashed through

the trees nearby. J.C. saw a massive shadow, and heard splintering wood, as whatever it was shuffled by and wandered off into the heat of the morning.

At this point, the realization sunk in that when he had come "again," he had actually showed up long before the first time—the exact opposite of "again," and plopped down in a large mud puddle somewhere after the late Jurassic period, maybe toward the middle Cretaceous, give or take a few hundred millennia.

The humans he had expected wouldn't exist for another few hundred million years, and now he was stuck here, ironically, without a prayer.

Book 2

J.C. **trudged through** the dirt, muttering to himself about sandals. He had almost left the remaining one behind, but decided to keep it, despite his discomfort, as a matter of principle. He could conjure up a new one, he supposed, like he did with his guns and ammunition, but to do so felt like a slap in the face. This place had taken his favorite sandal, and he wasn't about to give it the satisfaction of victory.

The ground had dried out somewhat, and the terrain was easier to navigate, as it became more rocky and mountainous. Up ahead, a natural opening in the rock shaded the surrounding area from the noonday sun. It would be a handy place for a rest and a cool spot to figure out his strategy.

Jurassichrist

J.C. slid down the rock wall and collapsed into an extended sit. He was exhausted from hauling the massive guns and equipment he'd summoned up across the jungle, and it felt good to relax for a moment, and get his bearings.

Before his problems with the flying creatures, he'd been poking around the clearing where he had initially landed, and it hadn't taken long before he'd gathered the attention of things that wanted to eat him. Various giants roamed the land here, and he'd had a particularly close call with some lumbering giant that looked like a cross between a Tyrannosaurus Rex and an emu, as it tried to sniff him out while he hid in the bushes. He hadn't felt so hunted since the Romans.

Luckily, so far, he'd only been sought after, and never actually found. J.C. was wily, and stealthy. He knew his luck wouldn't last forever, though, and it was nice to take a minute to breathe, here in this quiet, safe cave.

The calm wouldn't last long.

"Roooooarrkk." It was somewhere between the coo of a pigeon and the mumble of an ostrich, but much louder.

He peered into the darkness of the cave,

trying to see the outline of whatever had made the strange noise.

"Squwonk . . . chirrrrrup." A second noise, perhaps in response to the first. It was impossible to tell if it was more than one creature, having a conversation, or just some kind of animal that made a variety of noises. J.C. remembered his time spent in the animal laboratory, creating random organic parts and pasting them together to see what crawled away. (He was particularly proud of the platypus, which he'd created himself while drunk on manna, out of all the leftovers in the bin. The poisoned dew-claw was a particularly inspired bit, he thought, not to mention the fact that he'd stuffed them full of eggs.)

Could it be an ostrich? The ostrich mating call, he remembered, was a low buzz, a sound about as ferocious as the gasps from a dying vacuum cleaner. No, this was something far bigger.

Two heads popped into view at the end of the cave, as some kind of firelight illuminated the edge of the darkness. The male was larger, and had some kind of crest on his head, a huge bony ridge like a battering ram. The female had bright, wide eyes, who looked as alarmed as a dinosaur could look, at the intruder in her cave. The male threw back his massive head and hooted a strange honking noise, which led to several smaller heads appearing from somewhere below, where the cave turned down into the earth. The thing showed its teeth, and stood up at its full height, head just barely grazing the top of the rock walls.

"Shit." J.C. backed toward the cave entrance. Several of the smaller dinosaurs hissed like snakes and stalked toward him. Where were they all coming from? He counted a dozen or more, all smaller versions of the giant male, but still dwarfing his human body. Oddly, in the darkness, it appeared that their skin was almost feathered, with layers of bristles pointing backward, laying flat against their hides. Was this some sort of defensive quill? His finger instinctively went to the trigger of his cannon and he addressed the creatures. "I don't want to hurt thee. Stay back. Just calm down. I'm leaving now, and thou shalt be left to thine own devices. Steady. Steady . . ."

With a sudden burst of speed, the smaller dinosaurs leapt forward and hissed wildly, opening their gaping maws. A choir of fangs rose up before him, and J.C.'s fight-or-flight mechanism kicked like a mule. His finger squeezed the trigger and the barrel of the gun exploded, sending rounds of metal flying and mowing down two of the creatures.

The large male's eyes flashed with flame, then its cry echoed through the cave with a thunderous refrain. The thing reached down somewhere below itself with its front claws and pulled out a helmet. It looked like the bony ridge on the thing's head, but larger and more menacing, complete with spikes and studs that sparkled with an almost metallic sheen. The monster reached up and somehow slid its normal bony headpiece off, revealing a streak of reddish, bumpy skin. Then, the spiked helmet was slid into place, and the beast charged, plowing through the line of little hissing dinos and stomping toward J.C. He didn't even have time to fire another burst before the monster hit him dead center, sending him flying out of the cave mouth. He landed with a heavy thud, rolling over the dirt and rocks, before coming to a stop against a boulder.

"Owwwwww." He had clearly bruised the holy coccyx.

In the light of day, the creature was

enormous. Its new headgear lowered and it charged again. J.C. dove out of the way and the dinosaur crashed into the rock with tremendous force, splitting it in two. J.C. tried to catch his breath as he scrambled for cover. Now, the smaller creatures were upon him, and he tumbled backward, his hands around the throat of one of them, trying to defend himself from claw attacks. He felt jaws clamp down on his leg, and kicked, feeling the blood dribble down his leg like he'd been careless with one of his carpentry saws.

Summoning his power, he emitted a bright flash of light, causing the dinosaurs to wince and fall back, just enough for a cartoonishly large broadsword to materialize in his hand. He brought it around with a flourish, decapitating one of the smallest creatures. The largest dinosaur once again let loose an angry cry and snapped his huge jaws only inches away from J.C.'s face. His fingers felt for his belt loops as he brought the sword up again and again, trying to parry the deadly claw attacks. Finally, his fingers found what he was looking for. Without even looking down, J.C. pulled the pin on his smoke grenade and dropped it. It bounced twice at his feet, and then with a pop, began to emit a

Michael Allen Rose

cloud of white phosphorus burning with a brilliant yellow flame, producing copious amounts of white smoke. It was like a new pope had just been chosen, only inside a twenty-foot radius and not pumping out a Vatican chimney. This dense and nearly instantaneous cloud of white concealment smoke allowed J.C. to turn and run. Finally kicking off his remaining sandal, he sprinted hard, leaping like a gazelle over the rocky landscape. The gravelly texture ripped ragged edges around the holes in his feet, and he sighed, knowing he'd have to find time and water to clean them later. It was not easy, having perpetually open wounds, especially in a combat zone.

The dinosaurs were confused, stuck in the rapidly expanding cloud, and roared their disapproval, as J.C. bounded over a hill and took cover behind a cluster of ferns. He wasn't sure where to go from here. He had no map, no direction, and just a vague idea of what to do. From this elevation, he could see further into the jungle from which he'd emerged. Off in the distance, taller mountains cut through the trees like jagged shards of red glass. One of the tallest, a mountain with a crater the size of Nazareth, lazily smoked from its huge caldera.

He needed to find cover, before the dinos made their way out of the smoke, but where to go? Just then, on the horizon, somewhere near the base of the smoking volcano, a brilliant beam of blue light shot into the sky. It was breathtaking and bright, even at this time of day.

It was something to move toward, if for no other reason than to sate his curiosity. What could possibly make that sort of light? Neanderthals weren't even around yet, and dolphins, J.C. knew from the complaints they had lodged over time with the evolutionary committee, were stopped from controlling fire due to their lack of opposable thumbs. (In a landmark celestial court case, the dolphins had lost the right to bear thumbs in Dolphins Vs. Future Apes, which of course evolved later into the most litigious species of all, humans. J.C. personally thought it was an unfair verdict, but it did uphold the timeline. It's all politics, he thought with disgust.) Besides that, fire wasn't blue, and neither were volcanic eruptions.

Still wary of being hunted by the dinosaurs he'd intruded upon, he kept an eye out behind him as he slipped further beyond the treeline, fixed on the volcano and its strange blue mystery. The roars behind him sent J.C. running back into the jungle, this time seeking the strange blue beacon that had first caught his attention from beyond space time during his re-entry. He needed to get back home, and there was only one way to do that. He needed to hop on the crucifixion bus to shoot back into the place beyond space and time. Never had he hoped to find a creature with a set of working thumbs and an ability to use basic tools so much as he did now. The only way to get back, as far as he knew, was to find someone capable of nailing him to a cross.

Book 3

The trees thinned out a bit as J.C. approached the volcano, but passage was still difficult through the uneven terrain. His feet hurt, his shoulders ached, and the parts of his body that had been torn to shreds in the fight with the cave dinosaurs were itching like crazy as they healed up.

His mind was wandering. Dinosaurs had interchangeable helmets? It reminded him of those pesky Roman soldiers. How was that possible? Surely he had been hallucinating.

A strange sound broke through the ambience as J.C. trudged onward. It was a long, drawn-out humming, a sort of vibration that he could feel in the deepest part of his chest. The steady white noise thrummed at a frequency that J.C.

found relaxing. His stress dissipated slightly. (He wondered if this worked similarly to how, when they'd invented cats, they had installed a purring mechanic that vibrated between twenty-five and one hundred and fifty hertz, a frequency that promoted healing and improved bone density. Was this some kind of animal?)

No, it was far too massive in scope and steady to be an animal. Geothermal activity might have knocked a hole in the mountainous terrain, and created some kind of natural whistling cavern, perhaps, but the steady hum did not seem to be affected by the wind. Perhaps all the gunfire from earlier had given J.C. a case of tinnitus? But, he thought, that would heal up, theoretically, like any other wound that didn't completely obliterate him would.

J.C. pushed through a particularly dense patch of ferns and found himself stunned by what lay beyond the shrubbery. The forest had been clear cut for miles in both directions, leaving a wide path without any obstacles winding its way into the distance to each side of J.C.'s position, perpendicular to the volcano's peak far ahead. Upon closer inspection, though, the trees did not appear broken, cut, or smashed. The edges of the path stopped at perfectly smoothed and carefully sculpted tree lines, and it appeared that the plants had actually been coaxed somehow to grow at weird angles, jutting off to each side as though they were consciously trying to move out of the way to clear a trail.

It was as though the foliage had parted itself voluntarily.

J.C. dropped down and carefully army-crawled his way out into the open, staying as close to the dirt as possible. He didn't want to be caught out in the open by another dinosaur, as without cover, he would never be able to survive them if they came in greater numbers than one. He thought about the position of things in space and time. It was very different when inhabiting a physical manifestation. He could be hit by a meteor, without any warning. Life as a mortal was unsettling. But, following this line of thought, it suddenly occurred to him that he could summon up some kind of radar device to check for motion.

Slapping his forehead right where the thorn marks furrowed his brow, he was annoyed that he hadn't devised such a system before. His insides glowed like there was a bright fireball right in the center of his tummy, as he brought his mystical christ-powers to bear, and soon there was a small green box in his hand with a hard clear window, and several tiny green lights blinking away. It needed no battery, powered by Jesus-magic, and so he fiddled with the dials, making sure that each function did exactly as he had planned for it to do.

A large green dot stood at the center of the circular display. Emerging from it, a long green line spiraled around the screen, searching for any moving thing that wasn't in possession of the little device. A carpenter by trade, J.C. hoped that his creation skills were up to par. Electronics hadn't even been in the mind's eye of humankind during his last visit, so he was improvising based on some observations he'd made in Earth's 1980s. It was nice to be able to conjure up pretty much anything he could imagine, but of course it did get tiring, so he tried to hit the mark on the first try, lest he find himself underpowered during an ambush.

The little green box beeped a friendly beep.

BEEP.

"What's that?" J.C. asked, tapping the device on its side, quizzically.

BEEP. BEEP.

Two dots had appeared on the far right side of the circle.

BEEP BEEP BEEP.

Now there were three. In fact, with each pass of the line, there appeared to be more tiny green dots blinking into existence. Four, five, six, the number kept growing.

Then, J.C. noted with alarm that a similar line of dots was growing from the opposite side of the screen as well. He was surrounded by dots.

Quickly, he crept backward toward the ferns from which he'd come, but as he tried to lift the leaves to step into the shadows and hide, they resisted. He pulled and pushed, trying to climb through a gap, but the plants seemed to almost purposely tighten their ranks, and everywhere he tried to jam an arm in, an impenetrable wall knitted itself together.

"Lo, it is easier to . . . oof . . . thread a camel . . . ugh . . . through the eye of a needle . . . than to part these damned leaves!" with a mighty burst of strength, J.C. tore a branch from one of the larger ferns. Immediately, other surrounding plants rustled to fill in the gap. Apparently, this border was entrance only, not an exit.

The device was now emitting a steady BEEP BEEP BEEP BEEP BEEP. "They art coming out of the walls! They art coming out of the dad damned walls!" He observed conga lines of what appeared to be floating dinosaurs, heading his direction from both sides. Nobody had seen him yet, and his eyes rolled wildly around, looking for some place to hide.

Perhaps he could conjure up a disguise? But, he knew he was unable to change his size or appearance supernaturally. There was no way he'd pass for a dinosaur. He was just too human. He would definitely look out of place, and becoming a dinosaur snack was a far cry from the death by crucifixion that would get him off this planet and back into the ethereal realm.

Rocks? Too small. Trees? Not cooperative. He thought back to his training, most of which had been provided by 1980's action movies. Lo, through the grace of luck, did his eyes come to rest on the mud below him, and he had only seconds to enact his plan. He quickly covered himself in cold, fresh mud, wallowing like a demon-possessed pig, until he was covered from head to toe in the same color as the path. The two lines were now easily within range to see him, so J.C. gathered his things, piled them underneath his robed body, and closed his eyes, trying to match the behavior and general appearance of a muddy patch of ground. He didn't know if dinosaurs had thermal imaging, but it was a chance worth taking.

He grimaced as he tried to will his muscles to stay virtually still. He had to sneeze, and fought the impulse until he felt his eyes leak two tiny tears. The salt and mud mixture stung at the corners.

Now that he was face down on the path itself, the humming he'd noticed earlier seemed even louder and more persistent. With shock, he realized that the humming was coming from underneath the path itself.

Then, he felt the presence of the dinosaurs, and gritted his teeth. The hair on the back of his neck stood up as the creatures passed over him. Somehow, they were still floating, and he winced as he imagined one of them crashing down to the ground with his fragile human form underneath.

The bottoms of their feet and tails came within mere inches of the back of his head, and he could feel the wind of the appendages sweeping back and forth, just over his skull. The blood pounding in his ears did not quite obfuscate the sound from above. The dinosaurs, each in turn, hovering overhead, could be heard to be making the same humming as that from beneath the road. J.C. was the meat in a sonic sandwich.

Every nerve ending was on high alert. The sensation of the thunder lizards just inches from discovering his prone form was making his head buzz. The humming was incessant.

It felt endless. There must have been dozens of the creatures. J.C. concentrated on keeping from shivering, the cold mud having soaked through his robes. It felt like icy daggers dragged across the surface of his skin.

The humming lowered in volume, as the lines receded in the directions opposite from which each came. He was almost in the clear, but then, his ears registered one of the dinosaurs cease its droning hum. One huge, clawed foot settled down into the dirt only a handbreadth from J.C.'s head, followed by the other, next to the first. The weight of the thing actually shook the ground, and J.C. swallowed silently, to keep himself from choking with alarm. A tiny spurt of fear pee soiled J.C.'s robe even further, another annoying thing about being mortal he'd almost forgotten about.

Jurassichrist

The behemoth was just standing there. Right above him.

He felt it looking at him. Staring holes through the back of his head with beady, angry eyes.

Moving only a millimeter at a time, he slowly opened one eye and craned his neck around. He couldn't reach his weapon, which was pinned underneath him, without flipping over, the motion of which would surely alert the beast, if it wasn't already aware of his presence. He pictured himself, stomped into the mud, held down under a fifty-ton weight until he suffocated in filth, his lungs buried inside him.

The creature suddenly shifted, digging a furrow directly in front of J.C.'s nose with one of its talons. He prepared himself for the worst. The creature was straddling him, large enough to comfortably stand with its feet on either side of his mud hole. He was staring directly into dinosaur crotch.

Nietzsche said (or would say, when he was eventually born and did things, assuming that the timeline stayed intact) that if thou gaze long into an abyss, the abyss will also gaze into thee. Some other armchair philosopher would later add that if you stare into the void and it blinks first, you win, but the prize is insanity. Similarly, J.C. found that if you stare into the crotch of a dinosaur, and it opens its cloaca, not only does it feel like your soul is being stared into, but it also makes you want to die a little.

The gooey orifice swelled and transformed as it opened like a portal to a hell filled with alien genitals. The creature pushed, and a slime-covered oval began to crown, teasing its way out of the hole and getting stuck, just a little too large to comfortably escape from the now red-ringed, stretching vent.

The creature grunted and the egg pushed out a little further, a dome of white with red splotches only a few feet above J.C.'s face. There was nowhere to go. With a final groan, the cloaca swelled and released, dropping the egg straight down. J.C. got his hands up just in time to catch the huge sphere. The force of its landing sprayed albumen and blood into his mouth and eyes, and he grimaced, tasting prehistoric fluids. He shifted, trying to get into a relaxed position, as the monster took a massive step backward and he felt the shadows disappear from his face. He tried to think mud puddle thoughts as the huge dinosaur leaned down and inspected the egg.

Jurassichrist

Hot air shot from the beast's nostrils as it snorted and sniffed around the egg, which was now sitting upright in J.C.'s muddy hands. After a moment, the dinosaur reached down and picked up the egg with its claws, holding it up to the light. It nodded, apparently satisfied. As J.C. watched, the dinosaur leaned forward and revealed a strange cube of plant matter, which was apparently attached to its back almost like a knapsack. It manipulated the top of the cube with its claws, and deftly placed the egg inside a small slit in the top, then reattached the cube and grinned with razor sharp fangs. It moved as if to leave and follow the rapidly departing line of fellow dinosaurs.

J.C. froze as one of the giant feet hovered over his body, waiting for the crushing to begin, but to his relief, the creature began to hum loudly once more, and as soon as it did, its entire body floated upward until it came to hover a few feet above the path. Then it took off rapidly, in the direction it had been going before.

J.C. could finally breathe normally again, and he spit and coughed while wiping his face with his sleeves. This did little but spread the mud and goop around. This was ridiculous.

Fighting to survive was hard enough without being ill-prepared. He closed his eyes tight, and summoned some clean clothes, including a brand-new set of lightly armored, studded leather robes and some combat sandals. It was time to work a few miracles.

J.C. raised his arms to the sky and muttered in ancient Aramaic. Clouds gathered and formed thunderheads, and within seconds, the first drops began to fall. J.C. stripped off his filthy, torn robe and danced naked on the path, allowing the cool water to wash over him. It took a lot of Jesus juice to make the sky fall, but it felt like heaven.

When he was finished with his impromptu shower, he called up a hot southern wind, which blow dried his hair and beard. As he suited up, his thoughts smoldered. If these dinosaurs were going to attack him, bite him, shit eggs on his face, and who knows what else, then it was time to take the fight to them. He'd either find a way to get them to nail him to a cross, or murder the whole animal kingdom trying.

There were few options, so he ran in the direction that the egg-layer had gone. He could still see it, hovering along the path. How the

hell was it doing that? It had no wings, no
visible means of propulsion, just that weird
sound. A sound that was still coming from
somewhere beneath him.

The path turned slightly, and curve around
the base of the volcano, climbing a small rocky
hill. J.C. crested the hill, his gun pointed in
front of him like a divining rod. If there was
another pack of carnivorous beasts, ready to
give him trouble, he'd give it right back with
violent force.

His jaw dropped. Up ahead, the jungle faded
and the land opened up into a vast plain, the
volcano above overlooking it like a protector.
The crude dirt path followed the treeline only
to the bottom of the hill, where a grid of roads
topped with some kind of beautiful cerulean
blue material extended into the distance.
Sunlight streamed down, illuminating a
massive, golden city.

Everything was connected with cables and
wires of blue and gold. Huge towers bloomed
up from the middle of the city, leaving way for
smaller buildings with stunningly detailed
minarets and circular decorations. The design
was such that sunlight blossomed everywhere,
with holes and cutouts in many of the solid

structures to allow natural sunlight to pass through. In the middle of the skyline was a massive golden cylinder, topped with a gargantuan blue gemstone.

As J.C. looked on in awe, the sapphire stone that served as a centerpiece to this alien landscape abruptly lit up with a radiant light. The incredible beauty of the glowing gem momentarily made J.C. forget the danger he was in, and it pulsed, illuminating the golden spires surrounding it.

Hundreds, maybe thousands of different dinosaurs floated in every direction on the paths of the grid. At intersections, where he would expect crashes and battles between dinosaurs, somehow there was peace and tranquility, with each row of hovering creatures seamlessly threading and merging together without incident. Many of them raised their heads as the light in the middle of the city glowed. A terror of Tyrannosaurs broke ranks and drifted down the dirt road. Finally, able to leave the path, J.C. dove behind a large outcropping of rocks and waited for the trio to close distance. There were two large adults, and one smaller one, all floating along like it was completely within their rights to violate the laws of gravity. As they approached, J.C. noticed that the largest of the three had some kind of cylinders positioned over its eyes, made of the same blue glass-like substance he saw in the tubes and wires running this way and that throughout the city. All three were humming.

A massive orange flash lit up the sky. The dinosaurs all turned their heads, as J.C. clung to the rock and glanced at the skyline to see what was happening. The shockwave hit only a moment later, and then: mayhem. Dozens of the floating dinosaurs crashed down to the ground, a chorus of roars and screeches sung to the sky.

A cloud of smoke and fire erupted from somewhere near the middle, where the taller buildings stood, and one of the spires crumbled and fell. Blue sparks shot out from where the cables attached to it had been severed, visible even from this distance as a menacing glow. All three nearby Tyrannosaurs roared with surprise and fell to the ground with a trio of earth-shattering thuds.

As the larger two dinosaurs checked on the smallest one, helping it get off its back, J.C. used the commotion to slip down the path, unnoticed, leaping from rock to tree to culvert until he was right next to the grid. The roads were quickly clearing, as the giant animals began to panic and run.

Fire and smoke from an explosion meant some form of civilization, and since the dinosaurs were running away from the blast, J.C. figured his best chance was to run toward it. He would seek out the source of the madness. Anything that could harness the power of fire could theoretically use tools, like a hammer and nails, for instance. He scurried into the heart of the strange golden city, seeking a purifying flame, which was the closest thing to a beacon of hope he had left.

Book 4

Chaos. A massive pile of twisted, tarnished golden bits and pieces stood piled up around a charred base. Blue sparks careened around the wreckage. J.C. couldn't believe his eyes. The city was actually a city, complete with buildings that appeared to be lived in, although the stories looked a bit higher than he was used to. High ceilings could be sold at a premium, but in every single unit?

The time dilation he was experiencing confused his senses. Perhaps there were somehow humans here? But, he knew that time travel for mortals was impossible, so they couldn't have come back. Besides that, dinosaurs were everywhere, running around, snapping their jaws, roaring to the heavens. It was terrifying.

Was this the remains of an alien civilization? J.C. thought he would probably know if there were other sentient creations in the universe. Surely, his dad would have mentioned it.

"ROAAAR!"

J.C. turned and yelped. He had allowed the fact that he was awestruck by the sights to cloud his attention. Some kind of four-legged, spiked dinosaur with huge armored plates was bearing down on him. J.C. parkoured over a nearby chest-high wall and scrambled for cover, as the beast slammed into the barrier and turned it to powder.

"Get some!" shouted the lord, as he brought his gun to bear and squeezed off a massive volley of bullets. Some of the shots pierced the thick leathery hide of the dinosaur, but it remained unfazed, and with a turn, swept its spiky tail across the ground like a windshield wiper. J.C. had just enough presence of mind to jump forward, like the tail was a wave in the sea, in order to avoid being hit dead center. The tail sweep still caught his legs, and he spun head over heels twice before landing on his face.

Jurassichrist

The creature turned to face him and roared again. This attracted attention, as somehow, the dinosaurs must have known what the ruckus was about. Dozens of dinosaurs all turned their heads toward J.C. The chorus of growls, hoots, screeches, and cries was deafening.

J.C. felt the exhaustion creeping in. He really wanted to find a nice, quiet corner and get some sleep. Unfortunately, the army of dinos attacking him made that unlikely. He fired bursts of rounds from his gun, screaming like a banshee, waving it back and forth. The gunfire cut through more cables, dented golden walls, and took down several of the weaker looking dinosaurs. The huge spiked one once again brought his tail around, and slammed it down, causing J.C. to stumble backward and fall flat on his holy ass. He scrambled up into a crouch and plucked a fragmentation grenade from his belt. "I'll see you in hell. Literally. When I visit." He grabbed the pin, and threw the pineapple, which slowly rolled to a stop underneath the largest dino.

An explosion, a spray of shrapnel, and the creature backed away, screeching like demons. Ragged wounds had opened up in its

Michael Allen Rose

underbelly, and J.C. used the opportunity to target them with his rifle once more. He flipped the switch on his gun to fully automatic, and fired, slicing through dinosaurs like butter.

Many dinosaurs fell in battle, but they were always replaced by more waves. J.C. noted with alarm that the newest group appeared to be strapped with some kind of armor, made from that same blue substance. He fired a few times, but the bullets simply bounced off the outer layer and went inert.

Pain exploded in his calf. It felt like a razor blade shoved underneath the skin. He screamed, and glanced down. There, a small Compsognathus, looking like a cross between a crocodile and a duck, had clamped its jaws down on the savior's leg. "Get off! Get off!" J.C. tried to shake his leg, but the shark-like teeth shredded his leg like lettuce in a salad. The small creature was also armored, and J.C. batting at it with the butt of his rifle had little effect.

A strange roar from above them sounded almost like words: "Hold the terrorist, Officer Spingle."

What the fuck was that?

The creature biting his leg hummed through

a mouth full of flesh and suddenly, a blue glow burst from behind its tail, where the armor pieces met. The little dinosaur reached back and with one claw, retrieved what appeared to be a figure-eight, constructed from the same sapphire stone he'd been seeing since he had arrived.

The figure-eight phased through his legs, sending weird tickling sensations through his spine, and J.C. found himself unable to move.

"What's this? What—?"

A massive claw grasped him around the middle and pinned his arms to his sides. Another took his gun, roughly. He looked up at a very angry looking Tyrannosaurus. The terrible lizard was wearing some kind of extensions over each of its tiny arms, that gave it a much longer reach. The shiny, almost metallic claws also glowed blue.

"Now, then. Can you . . . can you understand me, terrorist?"

J.C. looked around. An angry looking crowd of dinosaurs all stared at him, waiting quietly. A few muttered and growled, but none of them seemed at odds, despite being a mix of different species and demeanors.

"Who's there? Michael? Dad? Who the hell

art thou?" He scanned his eyes back and forth, but saw nobody capable of human speech, just these endlessly staring, pissed off dinosaurs.

The dinos toward the back of the group parted like a field of wheat, and there was some kind of commotion from near the ground. J.C. watched, snarling in defiance, as what could only be the next torture moved toward him. The Tyrannosaur holding him picked him up and held him front and center, facing the crowd. From between two tall brontosauruses that had somehow reared up on their hind legs, towering over the proceedings, came walking a short, squat ceratopsian. His armored frill was decorated with veins of blue light, and he wore some kind of icon on his weird, scaly chest.

"That will be all, Officer Spingle." The tiny dinosaur licked the blood from its lips and hopped back a foot, still watching J.C. like he was the embodiment of deliciousness. The frilled ceratops looked up at the T-Rex and nodded. "Captain Thurly." The giant released his claw. J.C. struggled, but the blue shackles on his ankles made it impossible to move. He wobbled and fell forward, landing with a grunt. "What is this? Who art thou? Satan, dost thou tempt me with insane visions?"

Jurassichrist

Roars of displeasure and anger deafened him. The ceratops held up its front leg, and the crowd quieted. "Yes, I hear you: terrorist. Give me a moment. Let us hear what this mammal has to say."

Stunned, J.C. realized that the creature before him hadn't opened its mouth. "How—?"

"You are hearing my thoughts, mammal. That is why you are able to understand me. Whatever concepts or objects I think of are projected directly into your brain, and as you receive them, they are translated into a language that you understand. We dinosaurs often communicate this way to avoid misunderstandings between species and regional dialects." The crowd began to growl. One threw a small rock at J.C., but the ceratops raised a claw, gesturing for calm, then turned back to his prisoner. "You are lucky I am the world's foremost mammalologist, as most of my peers would have thought you incapable of basic communication and simply destroyed you."

"I can hear your thoughts?" J.C. asked, incredulously. This was a method by which he was pretty certain that only celestial beings could communicate.

"Celestial beings? I would ask you more about what you mean, mammal, but for now, let us concentrate on recent events. Given the circumstances, I think your information may be worth more than your life. You remain alive on my good graces, so please do not do anything to jeopardize our relationship. Let's you and I have a conversation."

J.C. stared at the dinosaur. The idea that these creatures were capable of complex thought baffled him. YHWH had always maintained that he'd put the dinosaurs into the evolutionary chain as a link between the lizards and the birds, otherwise, he had little to say about them.

"I can see that you're overwhelmed. Let's go somewhere more comfortable, and perhaps you'll be able to give me more useful answers about the attack on our city." The ceratops turned to Captain Thurly. "The poor creature is frightened. Let's take him to the Wrap."

"ROOOOOOOOAR!" The Tyrannosaur was even more terrifying with its mouth open.

"Yes, I understand your reservations, but if the information we glean from this mammal is useful in saving future lives, we must do all in our power to extract it. Try to be gentle." With that, the short dinosaur turned and strolled back into the crowd. J.C. was lifted into the air by Captain Thurly's mechanical arms and he found himself dangling over a blue glowing cube.

"I know nothing about any attack!" J.C. flailed wildly, but the grip strength was beyond reckoning. "I am a man of peace!"

If a dinosaur could look skeptical, the Compsognathus did, twisting its face into a sort of smirk that mostly conveyed cynical judgement. If J.C. had been able to understand the tiny dinosaur's thoughts, they would have read something like, "Peace, my ass, you stringy fuck of a mammal." Then, it pressed the side of the cube, and J.C. sunk into it. Everything in his world was blue.

The walls of the cube felt inflated, like they were filled with air, but the sensation against his skin was clammy, almost moist. He was held fast, only able to move against the thick material with great effort, and then it was as though he was trying to swim in gelatin. The cube quickly acclimated to his body temperature, and he was surprised to realize that he had no trouble breathing. It was like a sensory deprivation chamber.

Michael Allen Rose

He felt something lifting the cube, there was a feeling of weightlessness, and the humming returned, louder than ever. His stomach told him that he was in motion, caged, alone and confused, but strangely warm and comfortable. He concentrated on the gentle humming and the smooth waves of motion that the hovering cube sent through him. The cube ferried him off through the heart of the city, and before long, he drifted off, losing consciousness entirely.

𝕭𝖔𝖔𝖐 5

𝕵.C. awoke in a soft, golden nest of featherlike wisps. He rolled to one side, testing his muscles. He was loose now, unfettered, and able to move all his limbs independently. For a moment, he was back home, waking up from a strange subconscious dream state where he'd envisioned a dinosaur adventure. It took only two words, shoved into his mind like a shiv in the kidneys, to dissuade him of that notion.

"You're awake."

This was no dream. J.C. continued to turn and flipped onto his back, raising his head to look around. He was in a dimly lit, cozy, circular chamber. Tapestries on the wall showed intricate scenes of dinosaurs, hovering, eating together, playing with strange blue toys and gadgets. They were woven of many different colored plants, and shifted and moved whenever he looked at them indirectly, confusing his peripheral vision with fascinating transformations. It was like they were still somehow alive.

"You like the plantographs? They are pleasing, aren't they?"

The short, squat ceratops was sitting across the chamber, perched on a golden chair that bent and flexed with his movements. It seemed supportive and comfortable at the same time. His front two "legs" were actually used as hands, almost like hooves with clawed fingers on the ends, and he tented them thoughtfully.

"Plant-o-whats?" J.C. inquired.

"Plantographs. My decorations." The creature stood and walked casually around the circular room as he pointed this way and that. "Mammal, these show the history of our kind. Famous moments of our culture and our way. The history of a million years of dino civilization are laid bare here for all to see." The ceratops paused in front of J.C.'s nest, staring down at him. "My name is Myron, by the way. What do they call you?"

Jurassichrist

J.C. cautiously reached out and held his hand skyward, unsure of what sort of greeting was appropriate. "I'm Jesus. Of Nazareth. Although some people call me king of kings, lord of lords, lamb of God, Logos the Word, which is my moniker when I perform in rap battle competitions, light of the world, king of the Jews, rabbi, or Jeepers Creepers, but really I prefer you call me J.C."

"J.C. it is, then." said Myron. "J.C., what do you see in these plantographs?"

J.C. sat up. The nest he was in was akin to a bed, but made of the same transformative material as the chair in the room. It was amazingly elastic. He had slept like a baby, not only because of his exhaustion, but because whatever material it was made from was like pure liquid relaxation stuffed into a sack. He squinted, trying to see better in the dim lighting, studying the images. "Dinosaurs. And they're all doing things I hath never seen any lizard do."

"The thing they all have in common is that they show civilization the way it is supposed to be. Freedom for all. Love. Kindness. Dinos helping dinos, living in a world free of danger, sickness, poverty, and pollution. What you have done has disrupted that peace and beauty, and my aim is to find out what motivates you to act with such malice and reckless destructivity." Myron raised a small blue switch on one of the walls, and the walls glowed with more intensity.

J.C. could now see better, and he barely kept himself from falling backwards from his makeshift bed when he got a clear look at Myron. "You . . . you're covered in feathers!" Indeed, the certatops was coated head to toe in beautiful, silky feathers of orange and white.

"This is my true skin, mammal. I thought it might relax you if I were to be open and honest with you, perhaps make you more cooperative. I have shed my scale suit, and just want to talk to you, unarmed and without violence."

J.C. noted that his guns, ammo, and grenades had been taken. They had, thankfully, left him wearing his armor and combat sandals. At least he wouldn't feel naked during his interrogation, even if this Myron guy felt comfortable showing off his plumage.

"Now then, was that the only attack you had planned? Or are there more ambitious plans for us? Should we be on alert for similar attacks elsewhere?"

J.C. thought about his battles with the savage

dinosaurs he had met in the jungle, and then to his subsequent arrest and capture after the slaughter downtown, and shrugged. "Just the two, I guess? Art thou counting each individual death, or only the number of incidents?"

"Two?" Myron turned, his brow furrowed. "I am familiar with the one. What other attack are you talking about? Is there another bomb?"

"Bomb?" J.C. said, blinking. "What bomb?"

Myron sighed and shook his head. He was still communicating with his mind, so that J.C. could understand him, but a small squeaking roar slipped out. It sounded frustrated. "Please don't play dumb, J.C. the mammal, we just want to know if there is more than just the one. Are you part of a cell, or working alone?"

"I art here alone. This was supposed to be my second coming, and something hath gone horribly wrong."

"Second coming . . . another two, eh?" Myron paced. "I have a passing interest in numerology. Does this have something to do with the mammal ideology? Do you have a manifesto for us?"

"Thou speakest with confusing metaphors, Myron." J.C. stood now, trying to offset his growing suspicion that they were talking about two different things by physically moving closer to the ceratops. "What dost thou think I did, exactly?"

Myron pointed a claw, his face finally betraying some rage. "You set off a bomb downtown and blew up city hall! The Pangaea building is in shambles. It'll take scores of us weeks to tune the humming and get that building repaired. That's not even beginning to tally the lives you've taken."

"What? I set off no bomb!"

"Do not lie, mammal. What was that, when you were asking about all the deaths you caused?"

J.C. felt sick. Something was clearly amiss. "I meant in the battles I had before you captured me."

"Battles?" Myron said, pausing. Then, an unsettling shadow fell across his face.

"Yes, the fights. I was attacked," J.C. said, feeling the tension grow in the room.

"You're the creature!" thundered Myron, "We have had so many reports about you! A weird mammalian thing that walked upright and shot pieces of metal out of its arms. You murdered a number of dinosaurs. You invaded the home of the Redflooph family and killed several of their children before running off into the jungle. You tried to bait and kill Donjulius, the pterodactyl. He said you tied something around his foot and tried to ride him. Of course, it makes sense, that same mammal would come commit a terrorist action."

"I did not bomb anything, I promise you. I only fought the creatures—" J.C. was stopped by a look from Myron, who puffed up his feathers like an angry ostrich. "I mean, your . . . dinosaurs . . . because I was attacked."

"Of course they attacked you! You invaded their home! Foolish mammal, have you no decency?"

"I have plenty of decency! And I swear to thee, I never meant to hurt any of thou. I was not even supposed to be here today. I was meant to be about one-hundred million years in the future, somewhere in Jerusalem. Even Tallahassee or Chicago would be closer than this. This is all a terrible mistake. Please, you must believe me."

Myron looked J.C. in the eyes, and held out a claw to take the son of man by the chin, turning his head side to side. After a moment, he nodded. "I believe you, mammal. I think you meant no harm, but you have done much.

There are many dead because of you, and the less tolerant among us would have you destroyed before you spread your hateful ideas any further."

J.C. hung his head. "I didn't know thou were sentient beings. I have only heard tales of your savagery."

"Well, perhaps we can find a way for you to atone."

J.C. thought about his original purpose on Earth, and the troubles and tribulations of his first appearance. He thought about the sins of humankind, and his sacrifice, attempting to gain them forgiveness for being such awful pieces of shit. The very idea of atonement was a deeply seeded part of him, something he couldn't ignore.

"Perhaps, I can help you. I was known as a healer, once."

Myron nodded. "Perhaps."

"I need to get back home, so I can try again and do this right. The only way I know how to do so, is to get thy help. Dost thou have nails and a hammer we can build with?" He was met with a blank stare. He tried again, meekly. "Any tools?"

Myron's thoughts came through loud and

clear: "If I understand what you mean by tools, no, not exactly. There is no need for such things, here. We have the humming. It allows us to build all of our marvels in harmony with the natural world, but . . . there may be a way to help you. Perhaps, if you can help us figure out who was behind this tragic day, we can assist you in building your contraption and getting you back to your home. I believe that your primitive mammal brain may be useful to us, helping us think outside the box."

J.C. smiled. Finally, there was some hope.

Myron frowned back. "But, it certainly wasn't a dinosaur that did this. If you did not bomb the Pangaea building, then who did?"

From somewhere outside of the room, there was a sudden crash and the sound of shattering fragility. Myron looked up with a start, and stomped quickly over to a blue cylinder with small holes in its surface. He rubbed the top with a claw and spoke.

"Rooooar. Squonk rawr grooooop?"

A crystal clear answer came through from the holes.

"Garrrrrph. Rarrrooo!"

Myron turned to J.C. "We have a situation. Just a moment."

They were interrupted by a heavy knock. A round portal opened in the wall, and the dinosaur previously referred to as Captain Thurly bent his oversized frame and handed the mammalogist a large rock.

Myron noticed J.C.'s curiosity. "Thurly tells me this was just delivered to the Wrap. The Wrap is where we are now."

The rock was jagged and painted poorly with a red substance, some kind of smelly pigment. A small clump of hair dangled from the rock's edge, as though it had been recently used to bludgeon a rat.

"Hair. A foreign substance." As he studied the scratchings, Myron shook his armored head back and forth. "I think we have a lead." In poorly scrawled characters, similar to hieroglyphs or runes, it read "FEAR THE CENOZOIC RESISTANCE."

Book 6

The next few hours were a daze. A parade of dinosaurs came in and out of the small circular room, doing various things with, to, and around J.C. A few of them actually took the time to use their thought communication with him, giving him a basic idea of what was happening, although none were quite as verbose as Myron. They treated him the same way that a particularly kindly lab technician might speak to a rat that was intended for an eye makeup test later on that day.

All of them wore scales, though now that J.C. knew about what lay underneath, it was easier to see the almost imperceptible seams. The first dinosaur that came in had measured him using some kind of expandable blue rod, and had scanned it over his body until it seemed satisfied. From this one, he learned that the scale suits were multi-functional, to wit, they were used simultaneously for both social and physical reasons. They provided armored protection against physical threats and dangers, as well as being utilized for warmth and climate control. They also served as a modest token of civilized dinosaur society. Even the dinosaurs most removed from polite society wore their scales most of the time in public, and only removed them in the privacy of their own homes. That explained the family he'd done battle with in the cave. They had been in bed when he showed up. His guilt was ugly, something J.C. had never really had to deal with before. Although it was a very human emotion, he was used to alleviating the guilt of others, not taking it on himself. Was this what humans felt like all the time? He shuddered to think.

Maybe he was just "hangry." J.C. remembered the time back in Bethany he was hungry and lost his cool on a fig tree for bearing no fruit. Straight up murdered that tree. Then, stomach still a-grumble, he went off and drove a bunch of merchants out of his father's temple. If he'd remembered to bring a snack pack, maybe the whole devastating scenario could have been avoided.

Another dinosaur appeared, peering down at J.C. from the air. She hung upside down like a bat, but with long purple feathers around her neck like a mane, sticking out beyond the scale suit. She must have been some kind of medical officer. She would swoop in and out of the room, with various small gold and blue shapes. Some of them, she would tap J.C. with in various places, then she would make a face and touch a gold rectangle that she held in her talons. It appeared to be some kind of recording device, or writing tablet, far advanced beyond any papyrus or tree bark or stone that J.C. had ever seen.

On one of her visits, just after she had held two small blue squares on J.C.'s kneecaps and indicated that he should open his mouth and cough, he summoned his courage and asked her a question. "What is all this blue and gold material? I was a carpenter, and I have never seen buildings like these before."

The bird-like dino raised the ridges where her eyebrows would be, if she had hair. "The gold is orichalcum, of course. And the blue is ichor. We crystalize it with the hum." She rolled her eyes like she was telling a child why it was important to eat food to live. She then flapped away, leaving J.C. confused in his increasingly homey nest.

J.C. had heard of both. Orichalcum was a noble metal that had been mentioned in ancient writings about Atlantis. Ichor was the blood of the Gods, according to ancient humans, although by the time J.C. had first walked the Earth (well, second, according to this new, decimated timeline) the Christians had changed its description to a watery, foul discharge, in an effort to make the pagan Gods seem more disgusting and capable of being wounded. Was it possible that all those legends were based on some kind of truth, inherited from this, the first civilization?

This was, indeed, a civilization, though it pained J.C. to admit it. This brought to mind further questions, many of which his captors were unable to address. What happened to the dinosaurs and their civilization? How incorrect was the history he knew? And why was the son of God and one of the co-creators of life, the universe, and everything in it, unfamiliar with

any of this? He should have come across this
information at some point while working on
project evolution, at the very least.

Once they had completed his examinations,
if that's what they were, he was allowed to
freely roam around outside his little circular
room for a bit. They took him out of his nest,
and led him down a hall to a door that led into
a beautiful garden. Ferns and flowering plants
were bountiful here. He recognized magnolias,
barberry shrubs, and palm trees, which helped
him feel at home a little. Myron joined him, the
squat ceratops now dressed in his scales once
more.

"How do you like it?" Myron tried to smile
without bearing his teeth, keeping the
aggressive posturing to a minimum. He knew
how fragile the mammalian heart was, having
been the world's foremost mammalogist for
some time. Admittedly, most of the mammals
he'd accidentally frightened to death were
small, ugly quadrupeds with creepy grasping
hands, and a whole catalog worth of various
shrews, but this two-legged bipedal J.C. would
likely be similarly fragile, despite its obvious
evolutionary advantages, such as thumbs.

"It's nice. It doth remind me of home." J.C.

paused for a moment, feeling the strange split between his celestial and human sides. "Well, it reminds me of Earth home. One of them."

As they strolled together, J.C. caught a whiff of something cooking. His stomach rumbled, and the scent of food made him swoon.

"Hungry?" asked Myron. "Come, let's get you something to eat." Myron walked J.C. to the northwest corner of the garden where several small dinosaurs were picking strange fruits. Myron plucked two from a basket. They were small, greenish, squishy ovoids. J.C. tentatively peeled one with the edge of his fingernail, and gagged when the smell hit his nostrils. It was like a dog had shit directly into the hole of a cheese wheel. His stomach complained and twisted, and despite his desire to retch from the stench, he hazarded a small taste. The fruit was a little like a plum on his palate, with a nutty undertone almost like a chestnut.

"We call that ginkgo biloba. It's a fruit. New category of food. If it's popular, we plan to hybridize and synthesize many more. I have a plan for something called an apple. It came to me in a dream, and—never mind. Here, try some of this." Myron walked to a small platform of gold and took a packet of something from it, then turned to J.C. It was some sort of strange bread, with a weird green hue, and a small amount of roasted seeds. What excited him, though, was what he did recognize: a little clay pot of honey.

J.C. grabbed the pot from Myron and devoured it greedily. He hadn't eaten in what felt like ages, and any nutrition was good at the moment. Myron observed, approving. "You like bee vomit, I see. Excellent. We have an alliance with the bees, just as we do with the plants. They provide us sustenance, and we support their growth and lifestyle choices."

"Thou art friends with the plants?" J.C. asked, between mouthfuls.

"Of course," replied Myron. "Have you mammals not spoken with them? They're very receptive to reason."

J.C. shook his head, no. "I do not know much about what the mammals do. I am a long, long way from home. I have no affiliation with these creatures that are causing you so much consternation."

Myron sighed. "Come, now, it's time you learned of them, then."

Myron led J.C. through another circular door. This time, they ended up in a much larger room. Busy dinosaurs ran everywhere, touching various gold and blue trinkets and staring at flat panels of moving matter. In the center of the huge area there was an intricately detailed model of what appeared to be a landscape, projected somehow as a series of beams of light that met in a three-dimensional image. The light was visible due to a steady stream of light smoke or fog pumped from underneath the plinth on which the projection stood, and flowed out through a small portal in the top of the room, far above.

"What . . . is this place?" J.C. asked, amazed.

"You are in the Wrap, J.C. This is our central hub of governance." Myron escorted J.C. to the center, where a number of dinosaurs all stood, sat, and lay around the pedestal. One of them, some kind of Hadrosaur, pointed at various places in the illuminated smoke, growling and grunting. Myron roared, in a sort of throat-clearing way, and addressed the lot. "May I ask that we use thought communications, so that our guest can be included in this meeting? I believe he may have some unique insight into the mammalian agenda."

There were a number of grumbles and caws. One huge Spinosaurus, a massive, predatory beast with long, crocodilian jaws, roared in disapproval. Myron held up a claw. "Your dissent is duly noted, General Arius, but please indulge me. This mammal will be integral to formulating our best strategy."

The leviathan growled, but acquiesced. Even its thoughts sounded angry and reverberated the insides of J.C.'s skull. "As I was saying before I was interrupted by Myron and his pet prosimian . . ." General Arius brought his huge head to bear and stared red-tinted daggers through J.C. "Can you make it sit?"

Myron pushed a small golden bubble toward J.C. "This is really a desk toy, but I think it should serve as a seat. Stay quiet and listen."

"Now then," the General continued, "I say again, we must strike. Ferret these disgusting creatures out and kill all of them before they commit another atrocity."

A pink Hadrosaur barked loudly and scowled at the General. "That is not our way. We can't bring ourselves down to their level. That would make us no better than them."

The General snorted. "We will always be better than them, Counsel Rubella. Have you seen how they reproduce? They shit out their children, covered in slime and blood. There's no egg to keep them clean, nothing. It's savage and grotesque. Wipe out the lot of them."

Another dinosaur, a small green raptor, banged on the table. "None of that matters if we don't know what they're capable of. The mammals have never had the technology to do this kind of damage before. Something has changed, and until we know what, we cannot send dinosaurs into unknown danger!"

The room exploded into squabbling, with several dinosaurs fighting to roar over one another, until finally, the pink Hadrosaur named Counsel Rubella began to hum in a loud, unshakable drone. Immediately, the room glowed brightly, and waves of euphoria overtook J.C. He nearly fell backward off his bubble, as his muscles relaxed and his posture drooped.

Everyone stopped, and looked at Rubella, who apparently was someone worthy of their respect. Even the general was chastised. "This is not who we are. We are the bearers of the hum. We are the harmony seekers. We will not be made into monsters." She turned her large pink head toward Myron, and reached up with a front paw to slick back the few head feathers visible on top of her bony ridge. "Myron: How well can you control this creature?"

Jurassichrist

Myron looked down at J.C., who shrugged in return. "I think he'll serve. He has a rudimentary understanding of right and wrong."

Counsel Rubella tried to smile, like she'd just eaten something sour and was trying to keep it behind her bottom lip. She leaned toward J.C. "Will you help us, J.C.? I promise you that no harm will come to you."

"Fucking mammal," grunted the General.

J.C. frowned up at the kindly Counsellor. "I suppose I must. I feel that I've already caused you much trouble. But, if I do, can you help me get back home? It is a matter of cosmic importance."

"All right, good." The Hadrosaur stood up tall. "We need to find out more, and none of us can infiltrate the mammals tunnels. None of us, except him. We will send him to scout for us and learn more about the mammals' capabilities."

Myron smiled at J.C. "Get ready. You're about to go undercover."

Book 7

J.C. was naked, alone, cold and annoyed. Technically, he wasn't naked, but what he had on certainly couldn't be called "clothing." The dinosaurs had outfitted him with a skintight suit, that covered his body from the neck down. It was covered in scraggly, mangy hair. Luckily, the long hair on his head, and his beard, had been enough to convince the team that he needed no mask, otherwise he might have some kind of fuzzy rat nose stapled to his face.

A tiny gold piece of oracalchum with a blue dot of solidified ichor sat neatly inside his right ear. It was explained that he could use this strange device to remain in contact with Myron and the team back at the Wrap. He decided to test it out.

Jurassichrist

"Testing. Can you hear my thoughts? Are zebras white with black stripes, or black with white stripes? A pomegranate would taste really good right now. I could rub it all over my chest and it would be sticky and they might nickname me the pomegranate lord." J.C. shook his head back and forth. It was difficult to keep his thoughts focused enough to communicate only what he wanted to. The human mind was a dangerous and difficult beast to tame.

"Yes. We hear you. We will be monitoring your mind signal for any news. We will remain silent until you contact us."

That was reassuring. Any resource he could count on made him feel a tiny bit better about this. About an hour ago, J.C. had been dropped off on this mountainside, a dusty, red-tinged rock covered in sparse shrubs and desiccated vines. It was here, that the dinosaurs were pretty sure the mammals had a colony of some kind, even if they couldn't exactly tell J.C. how to find it.

He had been walking around on this mountain for a while, and it was getting cold. The sun was beginning to sink in the Western sky, fanning a cascade of red and orange hues across the wide mountain. He could see the volcano in the distance, and knew that he wouldn't be able to go back until he had done this favor for the dinosaurs. Besides, the walk looked long indeed.

They had transported him here via the humming, so finally he had gotten a chance to experience it up close without hiding in a mud puddle. Apparently, the dinos used the power of their minds to communicate in some way with the materials, the ichor and oracalchum, and their mysterious properties allowed for what even J.C. would call "miracles." The more dinosaurs there were in proximity, the more powerful the frequency would become, and so they had built this wondrous society through learning and refining their sonic techniques as a species.

Even the plants were affected, which explained the shifting flora he had encountered both in the jungle and on the walls of the Wrap. Whatever form of sentience that plants could muster, the dinosaurs had found a way to connect with it through the hum. Plants were used as borders for their roads, a decorative presence in their homes and places of business, and even as a warning system against intrusions.

Jurassichrist

The bottom line was, J.C. couldn't hum in the way that they could, so he was stuck here until someone picked him up, like a bratty teenager waiting for his mom at the mall.

He had climbed most of the way up the mountain, which gradually sloped upward to a squat, flat peak of red sand and dry grasses. He surveyed the surrounding area, and was dismayed to find that everything looked more or less the same. He thought about the thing in his ear and concentrated. "J.C. to the Wrap, art thou there? Dost thou copy?"

"Go ahead, J.C."

"There is nothing out here."

There was a short pause, as J.C. tried to maintain his focus.

"There has to be something. It's getting close to dark. They usually come out at night. Keep your eyes open."

In his frustration, J.C. had trouble keeping his thoughts clear enough to sign off. "It's empty! Blank! A sandwich! I hope there aren't any weevils here! I want to be back in a manger, all swaddled! Take me home! More sandwiches! Good bye, I'll be in touch." Psychic communication was most difficult.

He was now descending the side of the

mountain that he'd not been over yet, having reached the peak and seen nothing worthy of further investigation. The ground was steep at first, but leveled out as he walked, becoming more like a rocky plain. J.C. had to concentrate to maintain his footing here, as an abundance of sinkholes and divots had popped up in his path, threatening to break the ankles of the inattentive.

The plants here were also more ragged and chewed up than he had seen previously. Up ahead, he spied something different. It appeared as though several long, white objects had been arranged in some pattern. At first, he thought they might be wood, but there weren't any trees nearby, so the origin of the thin sticks remained uncertain. He struggled to see them in the rapidly fading light, but by now the sky had turned a much deeper shade of blue, and the stars, beautiful as they were, did little to illuminate his path.

J.C. tripped over a small dirt mound and swore, using his own name in vain. Trying to maintain his footing was impossible in the darkness, so he dropped to his knees and crawled forward, muttering under his breath about time and space and cursing both of them.

He was now crawling on all fours like an animal, still his knees and ankles found every divot and sharp rock.

He neared the pile, and was shocked to see that they were bones. The small bones were arranged in a circle, with several tiny ones sticking out from the ring like the arms of some kind of chaos sigil. This was not a complete skeleton, but a deliberate design, created from the remains of some little animal. He looked around for signs of predators, but then remembered that the apex predators in this world were the very creatures who hired him to be here in the first place. J.C. risked getting a little closer, and picked up one of the bones.

It was a leg bone. Maybe a femur. Judging from the marks along the edges, it had been thoroughly chewed.

"What in—"

The soil suddenly shifted beneath him.

With a yelp and a short scream, J.C. found himself falling, pulled underground through a shifting river of flowing quicksand, until, after a few moments, it slowed. He was sucked down through what felt like a small opening in the bottom of a natural cauldron. With panic, he realized that there was no oxygen here to breathe, and he frantically felt around for a pocket of air, knowing that if he opened his eyes, he would see only the blackness of the underground.

Finally, with a pop, he emerged through the hole, and then he was falling. His lungs greedily gasped for air as he plummeted a short distance and landed on a large pile of rocks, dirt, and other particles, and slid down the side of it into some kind of an underground chamber.

It was pitch black, and silent, the only sporadic noises made by remnants of the falling rocks. He listened in the darkness. Somewhere, water dripped, and sent echoes reverberating throughout what must be a fairly large cavern.

Something sharp poked him in the lumbar region. He reached back and felt around until his hand found another bone. His fingers travelled up its shaft until they came to an apex point where it met several more bones. It was a very large ribcage.

He was sitting on a pile of bones.

J.C. quickly got back up to his hands and knees. His back was sore, plus he was suffering from more than a few lacerations and bruises from his rapid descent, but he didn't want to idly sit on top of this death repository for any longer than necessary.

Jurassichrist

His fingers found the eyeholes of a gigantic skull. Whatever had died and left this remnant could easily swallow him whole, judging from the feel of its teeth.

Although J.C. could summon fire, he knew better than to do so when in unfamiliar surroundings. The last thing he needed was to accidentally light up an underground pocket of natural gas and end his second coming with a massive explosion.

Planting his hand on what felt like the top of a tusk or horn, he crawled forward in the darkness, but to his chagrin, the handhold wasn't solid. His wrist twisted beneath him, as the bones slid and another avalanche began.

This time, he was spared the fall, but being pushed down the mountain of bones by yet more bones wreaked havoc on his fragile skin, even with the addition of the hair suit. By the time he came to rest at the base of the enormous pile, he was bleeding from multiple cuts, scratches and gouges, and breathing heavily, trying to ensure that his lungs still worked.

For a moment, everything was, once again, eerily silent.

Then, a singular, small skittering noise in the darkness.

Michael Allen Rose

After a moment, another sound, almost the same in quality, but from another direction. J.C. realized with growing trepidation that the sounds were multiplying. Another, and another. The sounds grew closer and closer, creating a circle around him, only a few feet away in every direction. Then, all noises stopped.

J.C. listened in the darkness. They were surrounding him.

He heard a pair of jaws click together and apart, salivating, hungry, and very near. It was answered by a dozen more from all sides, and then, the sound became deafening.

Book 8

He felt their presence. Small creatures crept closer to him, gnashing their fearsome teeth and hissing warnings in the dark. They were circling around him like he was the eye of a tornado.

His eyes tried to adjust to the darkness, but there was so little light it was next to impossible. Something scurried over his left hand, and he pulled it back, yelping like he'd been burned. Something hairy bumped against his foot, and he brought it in toward his core, balling up in a defensive position.

For a brief moment, he considered summoning up another weapon, something like a gatling gun or maybe a flamethrower, but he considered his surroundings. It was too dangerous to fire blindly without any intel.

Something bit him, right in the side, grabbing an inch of belly fat with needle sharp fangs. It hurt, and he swatted at the creature, batting it aside. He heard it squeal in the darkness, and suddenly there was a rash of chittering from that direction. Another pair of jaws attempted to nip at his foot, but he was on his guard, now. He instinctively kicked out and heard the small creature tumble backward into the pile of bones.

Playing defensively wasn't working. Despite the risks, it was time to play the fear card.

Reaching deep inside himself and gathering a belly full of holy power, J.C. raised his arms like he was about to sermonize. "I shall descend upon thee with fire!" he screamed, as embers glowed at his fingertips, then a blazing tower of flame erupted from each of his hands.

The blast of heat and light illuminated the space. It was a cavern, with dozens of tunnels leading out in various directions. The pile of bones was picked clean, with obvious tooth marks and scratches everywhere. The crowd of creatures hissed and shrunk back from the brightness.

Jurassichrist

They were all mammals of some kind. Most of them were quadrupeds with short legs, long, pointed snouts, five-toed feet with claws, and long, hairy tails. Some had creepy little grasping hands, and even a primitive pelvis, but stood on their hind legs with difficulty as they scrambled backwards, away from the fire. A few had upturned snouts, with huge eyes and sharp, interlocking teeth that jutted from their mouths in a snaggled display of vicious natural selection.

J.C. stood at the center of a maelstrom. The mammals covered every surface, even perching above on some of the larger bones. He could see, by the light of the flames, that there was a primitive looking web of sticks and reeds far above him, and the creatures had obviously shaped the hole above the pile of bones to allow for their prey to fall into their chamber. The fragile net of dead plant matter would obviously hold the tiny mammals, but allow anything larger and heavier to fall beneath the Earth and be captured, injured, or killed. It was a primordial death trap.

With alarm, J.C. realized that all the bones in this chamber were previous victims of these creatures' hidden deviousness, and he scowled at them. It was tiring, keeping the holy flames lit, but the mammals were terrified, so he waved his hands back and forth like tiki torches as he slowly moved through them, toward the edge of the chamber. There was a slightly larger hole there, that might lead to a tunnel in which he could walk, and he needed options, just in case the flames' uniqueness wore off and the creatures regained their courage.

"Mammal . . . mammal? Not us mammal. Not tasty. Not good. Too alive. He make light light with paws. Hate."

J.C. realized that he could understand the chittering from some of these creatures. He heard whispering, gravelly voices from throughout the group before him. The chamber, he noticed, also stank terribly, and as he walked he realized that though this was probably some kind of feeding chamber, it appeared that these things also relieved themselves in here. If they were stupid enough to literally shit where they ate, who knows what other horrible things they might do.

"Can you understand me?" J.C. asked cautiously, holding his flaming hands out before him as a sign of warning.

"Bright . . . bitch. Stop it. Awful. Hot." One of

the shrewish looking creatures crept a little closer and hissed.

Knowing that he couldn't keep this up forever without draining his power, he found a tree branch that had slid down here along with the debris. He dipped it in the greasy dung that was piled up around him, and with a little assistance from his Jesus magic, he lit the end of the stick like a torch. The intensity of the light diminished, the mammals lowered their guard.

"I mean you no harm . . . er . . . fellow mammals . . . " J.C. slowly crouched.

One of the multitude, a rat faced, cross-eyed creature with a large scar across its nose, sniffed at him. "Not food. Who cares." It turned around toward the rest of its kind. "Who cares. Not food. Can't eat it. Who cares. Can't fuck it. No good."

"You sure not food? " screeched a small, beady-eyed quadruped.

"Does look like food to you? Is walking around all big, making sounds, too hairy, smells bad. Look at dangling stem! Weird lumps! Probably poison."

The little creature shrugged. "Eh. Cover in sauce. Seasoning. Not know difference."

"Is. Not. Food." The big one threw a rock, which hit the small one in the face.

The small creature muttered. "Okay, okay. Not food. You boss. Not food." Then it gave J.C. another onceover. "Could fuck it though, probably. Has holes, can fuck. Like shrub. Or rock. Or sibling. Simple."

"Talk is over!" The big one growled, sending the little one running for cover, and snarled at the group around him. "Well? What waiting for? Great ball of light in sky to explode?"

The foul, little beasts went back to whatever it was they had been doing before J.C. had fallen into their subterranean home. Some searched through the bone pile, coming up from the depths with small chunks of fat and rotten meat. Others began shitting, or fucking, or simply crawling over each other in the filth. They had almost immediately lost interest in J.C. and gone back to their most base and prurient instincts.

On one side of the cavern, a fight had broken out between two mammals. One, a weird looking anteater type, had its strange little fingers wrapped around the throat of a long, dirty weasel of some kind, which was biting the hell out of its assailant's long, warty nose.

Instead of breaking up the fight, or taking measures to keep the smaller mammals safe, the creatures nearby were shoving each other and hooting wildly, encouraging more violence.

"Fight, fight, fight!" they chanted.

Several of the others were scrapping over a hunk of putrid meat that was so old it had turned greenish brown. These mammals were disgusting. Now that he was low to the ground, he realized that he looked not terribly unlike a larger version of some of these creatures. The hair suit and the general filth and blood with which he was covered helped him fit right in here.

An expert in evolution, especially one of the architects of the concept, could see some unsettling parallels between these filthy, angry beasts and what they would genetically foster after a few million years. Physically, they were rodent-like, small and malformed, but the telltale signs were all there. Some were already attempting to walk upright. The greasy hair that covered them had been styled, after a fashion, with mud and lichen rubbed into it to create sculpted styles. They had proclivities for fighting, fleeing, feeding, and fornicating, all of which they were doing with craven, ribald enthusiasm.

"Excuse me?" said J.C. One of the smaller, less vicious looking critters sat alone nearby, licking its crotch in the midst of a lasciviously self-gratifying cleaning session.

"Busy. Fuck off." The creature continued to clean, drool and hair clinging to its chin.

"I just . . . I art new here, and was wondering if thou couldst give me some directions? Where is the toilet?" J.C. waited expectantly.

The creature barely acknowledged at him. "Shit anywhere. Who cares. Dumb. Go away. Busy."

J.C. crawled toward the largest tunnel entrance, avoiding rutting and biting mammals, all demonstrating the worst of evolution's darker side. He had expected animals with less refinement than the humans he had been used to, but not these revolting varmints. Although, as he thought about it, he remembered what humans had been like during his last visit to Earth, and shuddered. This behavior made more sense than he was willing to admit. Everything was backwards and upside-down from what he had always known. It was as though his own experiences were the only things that he could believe, even though he had helped set all of this in motion.

Jurassichrist

Earth's past had been filtered through some sort of psychedelic mushroom cloud of misremembered lies and confusion, but that didn't make any sense. He knew what universe he was in, there was no question about that. So, why were so many of the discoveries he made here so alien to him?

Exploration of this strange underground enclave might illuminate some new clue, and the only way to do so was to slip into the tunnels themselves.

"Out way. Fuck you. Who cares," snarled a small mammal that looked like a tiny, hunchbacked horse had cross-bred with a frowning coin purse.

"Sorry," muttered J.C. nodding. When he was satisfied that none of these crawling, mewling creatures were paying attention to him, he slipped down the tunnel, using his torch to guide him. He realized that these animals must all have some form of night vision. That was what allowed them to live down here in the darkness.

The tunnels wound this way and that throughout the interior of the mountain. Everywhere, there was wetness: mold, clumps of hair, feces, bones, and other squalor littered the tunnels, as though these creatures didn't give a damn what they did to their environment as long as their hedonistic needs were met. It was difficult to crawl through the tunnels, as they were obviously mostly used by creatures smaller than a human, but he was able to squeeze through most of the holes until finally he came to what seemed to be a central hub. Here, some very crude markings indicated paths leading to different places. He noted that the place he'd come from was surrounded by drawings of digestive topics, from eating to pooping, which made sense given what he'd witnessed.

Other burrows looked must be living quarters, with little drawings of sleeping beasts. Then, there were others that appeared to be brothels, or some other sort of breeding grounds.

The one that J.C. found the most interesting though, looked new and freshly dug. There was a carefully etched symbol above this most recent tunnel. It was a skull and crossbones with an explosion carved around it.

Book 9

Deeper and deeper, J.C. crawled through the crude, cramped tunnels. Everywhere, there was evidence of a society made up almost entirely of dregs. All chaff, no wheat. A class system comprised of a low class, a lower class, and a class so low that it couldn't be uncovered with a shovel and a sonar.

The mammals were principally interested in themselves and their most immediate needs—a stark contrast to the dinosaur society that he had observed a day's journey away in the volcano district—and they let him know it. Every time he passed another mammal in the tunnels, they pushed past him without pause. They didn't even do the typical back and forth human dance of "right of way" which even in Nazareth around the turn of the millennium had been a thing. They just plowed onward like their fellow mammals were piles of garbage. Since everyone did this, there weren't even any real fights, at least in these tunnels. It was more like the creatures were completely self-absorbed. It would take entirely too much attention and focus to care about what anyone else might be doing in the vicinity.

By the time he reached the end of the tunnel, J.C. was covered in filth, and his hair suit was drooping and sloughing off in places where it had torn in the fall, leaving him looking like a particularly patchy ape with mange. When he was certain that the coast was clear, he tucked himself away in the corner of a sharp turn and put a finger in his ear.

"This is J.C. calling the Wrap. Dost thou read me?" This silent way of communicating was useful when in an undercover situation. If anyone wandered by, he could just growl or smile or pretend to be masturbating and nobody would be the wiser.

Myron's voice appeared in J.C.'s mind. "J.C. Good. We were concerned, as we hadn't heard from you in some time. Where are you?"

Jurassichrist

"I am inside the mountain."

"What? Our reception is not very solid, I believe I heard you say that you were inside the mountain?"

"Thou art correct."

"How did you get inside it?"

"I fell through a sinkhole, into a cavern. Listen, there are mammals down here. Lots of them."

"Good, you found their tunnels. What are they doing?"

J.C. paused for a moment, trying to find the best way to phrase his answer. "Sinning."

"What?"

A pair of snorkel-nosed beasts wobbled by, giggling like fiends. They glanced up at J.C. who quickly tried to look nonchalant.

"Big one," said the one on the left.

"Who cares," said the one on the right. "Can't fuck it. Can't eat it."

They looked suspiciously at the man in their midst and stopped, sniffing. "What you do? You sit here why?"

J.C. struggled to think. In his mind, he heard Myron trying to ask him something, but it was all static in the moment as he concentrated on maintaining his cover. He shook his hair wildly

and stared at the larger of the two creatures. "Er
. . . who cares!" he ejaculated. "Fart. Buffalo
chicken. Pittsburgh. Reality television!"

The creature nodded. "Who cares. Fuck it. It
my hot body, I do what want. Next top model."
With this, it attempted to snap its greasy little
fingers, but the knuckles were not yet advanced
enough for that kind of dexterity. After a few
attempts, it raised a middle finger, seemingly
satisfied, and bounded off down the tunnel, the
smaller one tittering behind it all the way.

"J.C.? Are you all right?" It was Myron,
desperation in the voice of his mental
projection.

"Yes, I am well. I have been able to maintain
my cover." A symbol marked the end of the
tunnel, another passage stamped with the same
skull and explosion from before. "I believe I am
on the right track. Surely, this is some manner
of war room. I shalt explore it and be in contact
shortly."

"Be careful."

It was nice. Myron actually sounded a little
worried about him. J.C. had to wonder if it
wasn't unlike humans having a pet that worked
for their benefit, like a farm horse, or a police
dog, or a helper monkey, or a lunch lady.

Perhaps they really were invested in his safety. It would certainly seem to reflect the values of their society, as despite his massive evolutionary seniority, here he felt lower on the food chain, yet they were still treating him kindly even after his rampage. Like art lovers capturing the bull in their China shop and allowing it to live on a farm because its animal nature made the destruction forgivable.

A few yards further along, the tunnel widened out, and then abruptly came to an end. At first, it seemed like the tunnel had just stopped, with a dark gray slab marking the terminus. On closer inspection, however, the slab was far smoother than any rock. He reached out and tapped against it with his fingertip, bringing the torch closer. It felt cold to the touch, and he realized with astonishment that it was metal. Not a naturally occurring deposit, but an actual smooth, polished and shaped metal doorway. In the bottom part of the structure, a small wheel, placed just at the perfect height for the smallest of the mammals to reach, glistened in the dim firelight.

"What's a wheel doing here?" J.C. knew the timeline, he'd been over the specs, he'd watched and listened as humanity took the first halting steps toward civilization, hitting milestones such as the control of fire, domestication of animals, and yes, the invention of the wheel. Neanderthals were barely a glint in the eye of the epoch to come, as of yet, and here was a wheel. Even so, this wasn't even made of carved stone, but from what appeared to be steel.

Carefully, he turned the small wheel, which spun a few full turns before the door popped open with an audible click. He pulled, and the door opened on a hinge, another anachronism, and one more suspicious reason to be alarmed that things were not right. He crawled through the opening and found himself in a large, circular room.

His torch was no longer necessary. Although the room was carved from the same stone and soil as the surrounding tunnels, crude, circular light sources were stuck to the chamber walls like polka-dots. J.C. experimentally pressed one that was nearby, and the dome pushed inward with a click, turning the light off. Upon a second push, the light clicked back on again.

The room was decked out in a variety of strange, alien objects. Most of them were placed upon surprisingly well built and level

shelving units. Fascinated, J.C. crawled
forward to inspect the merchandise. He picked
up a device that had a handle ending in a weird
metal triangle. The words "fat magnet" were
printed on the side. Was this to remove fat from
food? Did these creatures not know that fat isn't
magnetic?

Nearby, a patch of artificial grass had been
cut into a rectangle. There were stains of what
could only have been shit, running up and
down the thing, almost concealing the words
"The Potty Patch." The next shelf held bright
orange shorts called "sauna pants" that would
apparently heat one's abdomen and genitals in
the pursuit of losing weight. Underneath those
was a shelf containing a variety of weights, one
of which said "shakeweight" and was
apparently designed to mimic the sex act of
manual gratification.

The room opened up past the shelves to a
small amphitheatre, filled with chairs that
featured a process by which the seat moved
around in circles, spinning the ass of whoever
was planted there. A tiny mammal, a sort of
"proto-rat" clung to one of them, squealing
madly, as he rode it like a mechanical bull. Two
others, like misshapen wallabies, cracked up,

holding their sides laughing, as their tiny friend threw up its lunch all over the chair, still somehow clinging firmly to the seat. These creatures didn't even have fully functioning torsos that would behoove them to sit in chairs, and yet here was a whole warehouse of "Hawaii Chairs." What was going on here? The three critters spied J.C. and skittered off down the hall, the smallest of them still wobbling and stumbling, followed by a trail of spit-up.

Then, he saw the screen. It was some kind of synthetic material, certainly nothing from the natural world. Drawings, scribbles, and notations covered it, along with tons of graffiti. Two things stood out. The first was "Cenozoic Resistance" printed in large, bold lettering. The second was beyond the screen. A pile of bombs and explosives sat in a large pile, barely sorted by explosion capacity and payload. Most of them had a layer of dust on them, as though they had been stockpiled here for a while, but there was notable evidence that something had recently been dragged from the pile, through the chamber and out the door.

"You. What do you here?"

A small, angry looking possum was sitting on one of the chairs, staring.

Jurassichrist

"I . . . who cares?" J.C. asked, assuming it was the password for social lubrication here.

"I care. You have shiny? Only shiny can go to here." The possum turned to show J.C. the metal badge stuck to its chest.

J.C. used a quick flash of Jesus power to summon a hunk of metal similar to the one worn by the possum and smiled, using it to reflect light toward the creature's eyes. "I am new here. Canst thou give me an orientation?"

The possum rolled its tiny eyes and snarled. "Me better get promotion for showing newbies magic time." The little animal jumped down from the chair, with a spinning flourish, and waddled around the room, pointing things out. "Better Marriage Blanket. Go-Go Pillow. Potty Putter. Ooh, this how me get hair so pretty. See Flowbee?" The possum slapped its paw on a switch, and the thing started whirring like a hornet's nest. Within moments, the creature's hair was sucked into the chamber where it was cut like weeds from a lawn. It cooed, enjoying the sensation.

"Where did all of this come from?" J.C. asked.

The rodent looked at him like he was an idiot. "If you brave enough to work in magic room, you be briefed. Yes? No? Stupid asshole boss. All things come from Tee Vee."

J.C. blinked. "TV?"

Sighing, the mammal led J.C. past the screen and back toward the edge of the chamber, beyond the stockpile of weapons. "There. Tee Vee. You been living under rock?" The creature wandered back toward the center of the room and hopped up onto its chair. It curled up and settled down for a nap. "Now, let me work," it muttered. "Working for weekend." It started snoring.

J.C. turned back to the wall indicated by the mammal, and saw a strange black box with what appeared to be a form of glass over the front. Faint images appeared on it. Every minute or so, the visions changed to show a different product, many of which were in this very room. In the corner of the screen was a logo "As Seen On TV" along with instructions on how to receive the items pictured.

The instructions read:

Pick item.

Want item.

Pray for item.

Check magic room.

J.C. had seen televisions before, in his

various observations of the human world throughout time, but this was very different. There was no knob or button to change the channel, just a steady stream of products "As Seen On TV," the only common factor being the utter ridiculousness of each item. There was no logo or brand on the screen, just a blank, black facade, and no power button. Someone, somehow, had put this here. It was as though someone was trying to give evolution a running start by pushing the technological development of mammals up by several million years.

Who would have the power to do that, and why? What would it possibly accomplish? And why choose the trashiest pieces of technology to ever have existed, even before allowing them to learn to use tools? His investigations were turning up far more questions than answers, and he didn't know how to get back out of here.

"Wrap? Come in."

There was no answer.

"Hello? Myron? It's J.C. I have unsettling findings we must discuss. Art thou there?"

His thoughts were his own, with no voice appearing to ease his concern or lend him support. On the screen, an invisible voice asked "Are you tired of rolling meat into little balls

Michael Allen Rose

yourself? Try Meatball Magic!" He wondered, if he selected something and "prayed," what the holy hell would answer from the other side. He was almost afraid to find out.

Book 10

J.C. was **whispering** in the darkness, somewhere buried in the middle of a mountain. He was dirty, tired, hungry, and thought his nose might have literally severed its own connection to his brain to avoid smelling any more of the foul miasma floating about in these subterranean passages.

"Please," he hissed. "Come in, thou must be listening." After visiting the room of the "As Seen On TV," J.C. had been unable to get his thought communications working. Every time he tried, his thoughts hit a wall of interference, almost like a bubble had formed around his mind and the thoughts just echoed instead of projecting out into the universe.

J.C. closed his eyes and concentrated as hard

as he could. He thought maybe whispering the words would amplify the process somehow, but it seemed fruitless.

"Hey. You big. Have thumbs. You want get drunk and destroy stuff?"

The voice from behind him startled him, and he turned toward a very small, gray shrew. It was obviously a runt, which was probably the main reason it was friendly at all, seeing as J.C. was big enough to swallow the little mammal in one bite.

The shrew was dragging around some rotting fruit, some kind of berries, and it staggered slightly as it stood, waiting for an answer.

"Actually," said J.C., "I would like to find a way out of here. You know, to the surface?"

The creature burped, shuddered, and leaned its tiny frame against J.C.'s knee. "Surface? Why go there? We on easy street now. No need hunt."

"No need to hunt? How will we eat?"

The shrew laughed and slapped J.C.'s knee. "You funny. Remember? We use products, become powerful, kings, dukes, earls, C.E.O.s. Wait . . . why you no remember? You new here?"

Jurassichrist

"Yes, I am."

The shrew regarded J.C. suspiciously. "Nobody that new. You big. You all grown. Where you come from anyway? This joke?"

J.C. noticed that the drunken mammal's rotting fruit was almost gone, and had an idea. "Yes, haw haw, a joke. Let us talk about it over some more . . . uh . . . fruit?"

The shrew kicked at his last few berries with disgust. "Happy fruit almost gone. Shitty. Need more fun magic juice, but too small. Other mammals kick my ass and call me booger."

J.C. shook his head. "How awful. I can't believe they call you booger."

"No, I get used to name. Thing Booger not like is they keep all happy juice and beat skull with rocks."

"Say, uh . . . Booger. Could thou lead me to a source of water?"

Booger narrowed his little eyes, and hissed. "You not even know where water is? You just born, big one? You stupid. What in it for me?"

J.C. smiled. "I can get you a whole lot of happy juice."

It took everything J.C. had left in him to keep up with the little mammal, even as inebriated as he was. As soon as he'd been promised more drink, the creature had scurried off like a lightning bolt, darting through the tunnels until they had descended to an even deeper level. The ground was warmer down here, far below the surface, but the air itself was cool and humid. Booger led J.C. through a cavern and they emerged at the edge of a large underground lake.

Giant stalactites hung from the ceiling and dripped cold water. J.C. crawled to the edge of the lake, cupped his hands, and drank deeply. The water was cool and pure, with traces of salts and minerals, but definitely fresh. His parched throat screamed with ecstasy as the liquid rolled down the desert of his esophagus.

The shrew hiccupped and tapped his tiny foot. "Okay, so what deal? Happy juice. I not drunk enough. Don't even feel like masturbate. Hurry."

J.C. picked up the shrew like he was carrying a pet cat. Booger half-heartedly struggled, but then the height and motion made him too nauseous to fight, and he muttered something about "who cares" and "better be good." J.C. deposited Booger in a large divot in the rock that had collected a quart or two of standing water. The shrew perched on the side of the lip, just above the water line, wobbling slightly. J.C.

concentrated and lay his hands upon the surface of the water. Booger peered through one of the holes in J.C.'s palm, as the water filled with red tendrils, then, with a burst of crimson, transformed entirely into a wine deposit. The mammal took a halting sip. His eyes went huge and he stuck his face into the wine, slurping it like soup.

"So, about that joke I was making. About not hunting. You were saying something really funny about that, I think."

"Was?" The shrew was visibly getting more drunk by the second, truly enjoying the wine. He slipped forward and dunked under the surface for a moment. A few bubbles came up, then the mammal pulled its head back out, took a deep breath, and made a "whooo!"

"Yes, something about why we weren't hunting. We were pretending we didn't know why that was so."

"Oh," the mammal said, falling sideways and picking itself back up on wiggling little legs. "I funny. Yes. We no need hunt because all things come to us through smart traps and soon we learn all products for great evolution. We just get magic from box and learn to be consumer whores, like announcer said."

"Consumer what?"

"As seen on . . . hic . . . tee vee." With a gasp, the shrew passed out in his naturally carved wine bucket, floating on his back. Fleas and mites jumped for their lives as he sank like the *Titanic* under the alcoholic waves in a passed-out blissful reverie. Only his nose was visible from beneath the waves of wine.

J.C. needed to get out of here and bring his intel back to base. Someone or something had somehow armed these creatures with bizarre items from the future and was manipulating them, trying to force evolution and shape the future of mammals. J.C. shuddered to think what sort of humans this path would create, considering these creepy creatures were already exuding selfishness, laziness, violent tendencies and sexual largesse this early in their development as the class Mammalia.

It took him a considerable amount of time to find a tunnel that ascended, or at least one large enough for him to crawl into without having to scrape through the corners by inching sideways on his belly. After many false endings and confusing loops, and more than a few encounters with his fellow mammals that infested these tunnels, J.C. made his way to a

main shaft of some sort that was nearly vertical.
An indirect reflection of natural light radiated
from somewhere far above his head.

"This must be where the oxygen comes
from," he muttered, as he looked around for
something to climb. Tiny claw marks and paw-
sized hand-holds covered the walls in rows, and
it was evident that this shaft was indeed
something that could be climbed, but not by
something as big as a man.

He tested one of the hand-holds, and it
crumbled beneath his fingertips as soon as he
put any pressure on it. He tried using his
thought communication to reach out, but again,
it felt like his ears were stuffed with cotton, and
no response came. He had to get out of here,
but how?

Even if he conjured up a rope, he wasn't sure
how he was supposed to get it all the way up the
shaft, much less secure it to something that
would hold his weight. Climbing gear was a
risk, especially considering his weight and the
loose soil in the tunnels. He was pretty sure he
could survive being buried alive, but what
would he do then?

There was one thing left to try, and it would
take a miracle.

The last time he'd done this, it had taken nearly forty days to gather up enough power to pull it off. Of course that time, he had a lot further to go.

It was forty days after his resurrection when he finally got to go home, but of course to maintain the story he'd been living for so many human years, some theatricality had to be involved. Hopping across the planar dimensions to get home was a simple act of matter transference and time displacement with a twist of chrono-spatial looping and a smidgen of reality bending. (Reality bending, for the record, is like the art of glass blowing, only imagine that the glass is the matter that binds the universe together, and the tragedy when a glass blower gets molten glass in his eyes is metaphorically the end of existence as we know it.) But in order to wow the crowds, as well as maintain their very basic understanding of the message behind the whole stunt, J.C. had chosen to ascend, physically.

The direction didn't matter, because up doesn't really exist. Everything exists in space as relative to everything else, and the only reason humans think of up as "up" is because they can barely conceptualize the force of gravity, much less the fourth dimension.

Jurassichrist

His pals the disciples even had trouble with the concept: they had believed in a three-part cosmos with the heavens above, a flat earth centered on Jerusalem in the middle, and the underworld below. So when he went home, he decided to travel "up."

He floated up, blessing and blowing kisses, until he had penetrated the cloud layer and he was absolutely sure nobody could spy him phasing out of reality and changing his material form. It had been exhausting, but necessary.

Now, he was going to attempt the same trick to get out of a hole. At least he didn't have to reach the fucking troposphere this time. He raised his arms like he was strapped to an invisible crucifix and concentrated. After a few moments, a holy light engulfed his body and his feet lifted off the ground.

"What the shit." A tiny voice made him open his eyes. J.C. looked down at two small, ugly, long-snouted quadrupeds staring in amazement as he floated upward. "Big mammal fly. Him secret bird! Kill!"

J.C. tried to concentrate as clumps of mud, shit, and gravel flew through the air. The creatures pelted him with all the detritus they could find, while screaming threats and insults.

Soon, there were more of them, all throwing shit and hooting wildly.

"Keep it together, J.C." he thought, as a wad of something sticky hit him square between the eyes. "Just a little further."

After what felt like an interminable amount of time, he finally rose high enough to see an opening. A horizontal shaft cut into the mountain at the top of the vertical one, hidden by tall grasses. Heaving with effort, he stopped hovering and pushed himself forward to grab the ledge and pulled himself up. Noises of rage and confoundment bubbled up from below, as the mammals prepared to chase him down. Now that they thought he was a bird, he was the enemy. It no longer mattered that he was undercover. He tore his now completely ruined hair suit from his body and ran out the tunnel's exit, stark naked.

The night air was cool, and he immediately regretted his decision, when a beautiful golden light surrounded him. A large blue vehicle appeared looking a bit like an ark, or some kind of war ship, only it was made of oracalchum. A hatch opened in the bottom, and he recognized the faces of Myron and General Arius. The general reached out an enormous clawed hand and roared so loud the ground shook.

"What?" J.C. asked, his long hair blowing in the cold wind.

General Arius roared angrily and J.C.s thoughts were invaded by a soul shakingly loud "GET IN!"

Behind him, emerging from holes all over the mountain, mammals poured forth, nipping and scratching at the air, screaming bloody murder. "Kill bird! He friends with lizards! Kill!" Just before they reached J.C., the terrifyingly large General Arius leaned his bulky frame out from the hatch and grabbed J.C. around the midsection, tossing him into the ship.

J.C. rolled and crashed against a wall, and the last thing he saw before falling into a much needed sleep was Myron pressing a golden button and the panel quickly sliding closed, as the ship turned in the air and travelled back toward the relative safety of the Wrap.

Book 11

He dreamed of Gethsemane. Gethsemane, the urban garden at the foot of the Mount of Olives in Jerusalem, where he had walked and prayed and his disciples had slept the night before his crucifixion. He had often liked to hang out there, once he'd grown to adulthood. It was peaceful, and the olive trees there were ancient and beautiful and covered in plump, juicy olives, ripe for plucking. It was in that very garden, during his first coming, that he'd gotten cold feet. He had cried out to the sky, "My Father, if it is possible, let this cup pass me by," but gotten no response. No, his cup had been filled for him and he had to drink it.

But now, in his dreams, the garden wasn't a

place of anguish. He heard happy music on the wind, and around every corner, the colors seemed brighter, the sun warmer, and the music more jubilant. The olives were fully ready to pick, and so he strolled between the trees, plucking the plumpest and most perfect drupes he could find and popping them into his mouth. But, he quickly noticed, olives were not the only stonefruit here. Soon, apricots, peaches, cherries and so many more were blooming from the trees, even as he watched, creating forests of edible fruits from thin air. He picked and ate, rapidly filling his aching guts.

It occurred to him that he hadn't eaten anything, but that thought floated away as he spied some old friends, lounging in the garden. It was a cluster of his disciples, the gang from the old days that he'd always enjoyed partying with.

"Matt! Lukey! John-boy! What is up?" he said, floating toward them, but as he got closer, he noticed that they were all asleep. "Can't you guys stay awake for even an hour? Seriously! Wake up!" Finding all of them asleep was a painful reminder of that night in the garden before his final act. He reached down and shook his bestie, Mary "The Baddest Bitch on the Planet" Magdalene. "Mary? Hello?"

None of them moved. From behind, a child laughed. Something darted into a bush. Then, from the opposite direction, another unsettling peal of laughter, and again, when he turned, the motion blur told him something was hiding.

J.C. crept up to the bushes, and parted them, but there was nothing there. The sky darkened, and the music took on an odd quality, like the instruments had been bent and twisted.

Identical bushes had somehow sprouted up behind him as he spun once again, obscuring the sleeping bodies of his friends. "They're dead, you know." Someone had whispered directly into his right ear. J.C. turned, with a karate chop, but his fist caught nothing but cold, empty air.

The giggles began anew, and this time he saw tiny mammals. Bent mice with primitive torsos attached to lanky, wobbling legs. They were darting between the bushes.

"Hey, get out of here!" shouted J.C. while watching the mice crawl over the pile of his sleeping friends. Now, though, all the facial features had changed, and instead of disciples and followers from his time as a human, they were distinctly becoming dinosaurs. Still, the mammals swarmed over them. J.C. shouted, and ran toward the scene to try and help his friends, and as he did, his body slowed down until it was like he was running through a pool of molasses. Every time the creatures came out of the bushes, they were changing. It was small things at first, but as they continued to run back and forth, things the size and complexity of mice became rabbits, which became pigs, which became kangaroos, which became tigers, and so on, until a motion blur of rapidly evolving mammals had completely obscured his view of his friends and allies.

Now, between the shrubs, it was a river of apes and monkeys, all of them turning their heads to stare and grin at J.C. When he finally fought through the time distortion and got close enough to reach out and physically interfere, the flow of evolving mammals stopped abruptly. His friends, disciples, dinosaurs, whatever they were, lay before him.

They were nothing but bones, their picked-over skulls frozen in malicious rictus grins. From the bushes, a rustle, and then: humans. A group of naked humans stepped out. They were sneering, eyes filled with evil intent. They spoke as one, directing their ire at J.C. "We told you. We are the dominant species on the planet.

They will all die. You are of us. Be one with us. Stop rebelling against what will be. Do you remember what happened the last time you wore the title of rebel?"

Surrounding him, the humans bit and gnawed at J.C.'s body. All he could do was look down and watch as his body unraveled into bits of bread, the blood shooting from his bite wounds and hitting the air as wine. His assailants were getting fat and happy, eating, drinking, and dancing, as the world faded out. A loud voice echoed through his head: "Buy now, only twenty-nine ninety-five! Become smarter, better, faster. Evolve today! Operators are standing by!" The last image that flashed before his eyes was a skull suspiciously like Myron's that had been burned and scorched until it was covered in a layer of ashes.

J.C. woke up with a start. He propped himself up with his elbows, breathing heavily, heart pounding. He was inside the strange blue ichor ship, the gentle whirring of the mechanisms that allowed it to fly working away somewhere beneath his body. He could feel the vibrations and the warmth, and if he listened closely, evidence that some dinosaurs were humming not too far away. Some kind soul had covered him with a woven blanket made of fuzzy reeds, and he relaxed when he realized that he'd only been dreaming.

"OUR MAMMAL IS AWAKE." The roar of the General did nothing to relieve his anxiety, but it did sound like the monster was trying to temper his usual vitriol.

Myron and two smaller dinos, a couple of Compsognathus who were both wearing bright golden scale suits, came to J.C.'s side. The two compys poked strange blue and gold implements around J.C.'s body, prodding his soft parts and making noises like "hmmm" and "unnngh." Myron patted J.C.'s arm with his large paw-like extremity. "Don't mind Schpungle and Dootmar, they're just checking your vitality and medical condition. We want to ensure that your time with the mammals didn't harm you in any way."

The ceratops helped J.C. sit upright, placing a soft golden rectangle with the consistency of a marshmallow behind his back. J.C. settled in, trying to ignore the weird probing happening on both sides. "Thank you."

"So, please, tell me everything. What did you see? Did you find anything that might explain the bombing?"

"I most certainly did," said J.C., suppressing a giggle as the compy wiped a spinning oracalchum tool across his undercarriage. "They have bombs. Weapons. All kinds of technology down there, the likes of which I've never seen. Not even in the far flung future of approximately four Anno Domini." (Although technically the designations of B.C. and A.D. were not used at the time of his first coming, J.C. had watched quite a bit of human development from his place back in the celestial plane, so he had familiarized himself with many modern concepts such as sealing wax, spaghetti, and podcasts. He had been particularly interested in the golden age of the sitcom, which is why the "As Seen On TV" icon and phrasing really stuck in his craw and unsettled him, like a puzzle with several pieces missing.)

"Bombs? But, how is that possible? We've watched as the mammals have begun their development over the past million years or so. They haven't figured out fire, much less how to pack it into a container for later release."

"We need to destroy them before they destroy us." General Arius revealed himself, stepping forward from the shadows. The extremely tall ceilings in the ship still barely allowed the massive Spinosaurus to stand upright. "If they have developed weapons of mass destruction, they will not hesitate the use them. They lack the moral compass."

J.C. absentmindedly nodded. He would never encourage murder. Thou shalt not kill, and all of that. But, he had seen the craven creatures below, and expected that the General was right. More explosions would soon follow.

Myron looked very concerned. "But how they did get these things?"

"There's a television down there. A screen that gives them ideas and items to use."

"You mean like our light projections?" the General asked, gesturing to the information screens at the front of the craft. J.C. noted that they were similar to those back at the Wrap, a harmonious collage of colored lights that created symbols and characters.

"Like those yes, but, this is a box that you plug in and receive channels from . . . " As he spoke, his mouth went dry. There had been no outlet in that room. No electricity. No cables or wires. That meant that the technology couldn't possibly work with the apparatus found on Earth. It had to be powered by magic. And there

was only one place he knew of that magic
existed.

"J.C.?" Myron asked.

J.C.'s eyes widened. "I have to get back
home. Now!"

Book 12

𝕵.C.'s mind was racing. Why hadn't it occurred to him before? The only way the technology to force and shape the mammal evolution could exist here was through celestial intervention. Someone was exporting contraband from another plane of existence for the sole purpose of changing the timeline, and that meant someone was motivated enough to risk the wrath of the almighty and being eternally, unrelentingly damned.

If there was a traitor to the evolutionary plan for Earth, YHWH needed to know about it before things took a seriously dark turn.

Screwing with the past was a serious no-no. He was already concerned about the various deaths and other events he had been part of while here in the Cretaceous. But even a few massacres were nothing compared to changing the evolutionary timeline by millions of years for entire kingdoms of lifeforms. The consequences of such a shift in reality would be absolutely staggering. In fact, if things went completely awry, it could affect even his life, despite his extra-chronological status. His first visit to Earth might take a completely different turn. Humans might have evolved into something wholly other, and J.C. wouldn't even have the same body. Instead of crucifixion, they might have killed him by shooting him into space from a giant slingshot made of liquid metal or something. Instead of twelve disciples, he might have been followed around by a shoal of sentient air-swimming flying fish, all named Horatio. It was impossible to tell, and that's why he needed to get back and uncover the wrench before the gears stopped turning entirely and the whole machine fell apart.

Since impressing upon the dinosaurs how important it was that he follow up on these avenues, they had been working to come up with a solution for his problem: namely, how to get back home. He suggested that they find someone who had explored the world: been around the block a time or two, and Myron started barking orders to the crew. They had passed the Wrap entirely, and were on their way across the volcano itself. Below them, the caldera boiled with molten lava and coughed out charcoal gray clouds of deadly smoke.

"Art thou sure we need travel over the volcano?" asked J.C. Even his mostly death-proof avatar wouldn't be able to comfortably survive a fall into a live volcano. Melting was one of the worst fates to try and regenerate flesh from, in the aftermath of an accident.

"It's the fastest way to where we're going," Myron answered.

The interior of the ship was eerily quiet, all the dinosaur crew humming to try and maintain the power supporting their flight. Falling under normal circumstances would be a tragedy, but above this massive bowl of flame and ash, it would be unthinkable.

"Where didst thou say we were going, again?"

Myron pointed out the strange, clear front panel of the craft. "To the rim of the caldera, on the other side of the city. We need to see the hermit, Eoraptor."

Eoraptor. The name made the other dinosaurs twitch and shuffle their clawed feet. His name meant "dawn thief," and nobody quite knew where it had come from. Some said that he lived up to it by rarely being out during the day, with other legends telling tales of how he was so ancient that he had actually figured out how to control time and stop the dawn from coming at all. Eoraptor was the oldest dinosaur known to Myron and his society, and from what he told J.C. everyone was simultaneously respectful and terrified of the ancient dinosaur. Rumors even held that he had been around since the dawn of creation itself, or at least the early Triassic, which was still pretty impressive.

J.C. couldn't remember much about the creation of the dinosaurs, but there were a few mortals that had tapped into the celestial realm in various ways and become something more. In the canonical timeline, the one he was trying to protect, there had been individuals that had discovered magical artifacts like the holy grail, the ark of the covenant, and the Batmobile. They had transformed into hybrids of the clay vessels made flesh that his kind had set in motion and the timeless entities that were his brethren. Perhaps this Eoraptor had found a way to commune with the heavens. Or perhaps, he was a kook.

"There." The ship landed carefully on a flat piece of rock. They were only a few yards from the edge of the volcano's interior drop, and the heat was intense. A few meters away, there stood a small house carved of rocks, with symbols carved into the sides and front. As the dinosaurs and J.C. disembarked, a stone door rolled aside from the structure and a small raptor peered out at the landing party from inside.

It was a small, lightly-built dinosaur that stood on two long legs. Eoraptor came into the light and revealed a three-foot-long body that moved with agility, despite its reported age. It had a long head with dozens of small, sharp teeth, and five fingers on its grasping hands with two of the fingers on each hand being very small. It looked like it would have trouble holding a bowling ball.

"What is it?" Eoraptor sent to the group. Its mental projection sounded strong and wise, and it made J.C.'s head feel swimmy when it invaded his mind.

"This mammal needs your help," Myron communicated.

"And why, pray tell, should I help a mammal?" Eoraptor sniffed at J.C. who tried to look nonchalant.

"Please, I need to find someone capable of nailing me to a cross so I can get back home. It's urgent."

The ancient dinosaur considered the human before him. "I have been through countless waves of evolution. I have been alive for millions of years, and I have never seen anything quite like you."

"Millions?" J.C. asked. "How is that possible?"

The raptor was still staring, then suddenly, it broke eye contact. "It couldn't be, could it? Wait here."

The contingent stood around awkwardly while Eoraptor searched for something in the back. The sounds of clutter being sifted through and crashing about drifted out of the tiny hut, until, after a few minutes, Eoraptor returned with a golden cross that was glowing brightly with an eerie, supernatural light.

The collected dinosaurs roared and screeched. A few actually unfastened their scale suits and ruffled their feathers. The energy that the cross put out was palpable. General Arius roared, then caught himself, using his psychic hum to ask, "What the pterodactyl turds is that?"

"I knew this thing was acting funny." Eoraptor held tight to the large golden idol and as it approached J.C. it glowed even brighter, almost vibrating out of the grip of its possessor. "It started glowing a couple of days ago, but I wasn't sure what it meant until just now."

J.C. reached out and touched the cross. Everyone jumped as a large spark of energy leaped from his finger to the golden surface of the artifact. "Where . . . how did you get this?"

"That's an odd story. A few hundred million years back, I was born weird. I didn't quite fit in with the family, since they had only really emerged from the water to breathe through lungs a few generations before, whereas I took to the land like a champion. I did a lot of digging, playing in the dirt, enjoying having lungs instead of gills. One day, I came across this giant letter 't' deep in the ground, and sure enough, my brain opened up and I started thinking the strangest thoughts. It spoke to me directly, almost. Put all kinds of images in my brain. For some reason, I haven't died. I mean, everyone else did. Kept living, and dying, living, and dying, generation after generation, but I just kept living, and it would show me things. Showed me you, for example, mammal. I didn't recognize you as the mammal from the visions at first, but the more I looked, well, it became clear."

J.C. was listening, but he was more interested in this golden cross. He inspected it closely, and his suspicions were confirmed. "This is a piece of creation. This is celestial. A stave of evolution! Someone must have left this behind by accident. We can use this!"

He had a vague recollection of the earliest parts of the creation project. He had used tools just like this one in the making of the universe. Had he somehow left this behind for himself? J.C. wished he could remember, but his prophecies and memories sometimes crossed streams, and any differences between past and future were almost imperceptible.

The team went into action. Loose teeth from the carnivores became nails, and following J.C.'s directions, they strapped him to the golden cross. General Arius was easily strong enough to pull the crucifix upright, and soon, J.C. was ready. This wasn't the traditional way, but crossing his fingers, he hoped it would do the trick.

Jurassichrist

"Everyone, just sit tight. I'll be back as soon as possible, so we can set things right."

As the dinosaurs watched, J.C. mumbled some magic words. A tall Hadrosaur, using one of the arm extender machines so popular with the upright dinos, carefully hammered the teeth through the pre-existing holes in J.C.'s palms, and suddenly his body went limp. An astral projection of him shot out of his human shell, and with a wink and a wave, J.C. blasted skyward. The dinosaurs watched until he was so far away, he looked like a star in the sky, and finally, he winked out of existence entirely.

"I hope he knows what he's doing," thought Myron, as the dinosaurs boarded their craft.

J.C. hoped this as well. He felt his matter shift and he braced for impact, wondering what he might find in heaven.

Book 13

B **wow-chicka bum brrum**.
Tap tap tap.

His fingers automatically tapped along, as he slowly regained feeling in them.

Tikka-tikka doo doo doot, bwahhh. A-doo doo ding dooooo.

Inoffensive hold music told him he was alive.

J.C. opened his eyes, one at a time. Slowly, the waiting room came into focus. All white, with large comfy chairs, and a variety of otherworldly beings waiting for processing. A large poster on the wall showed YHWH winking and pointing at the observer, with a caption that read "Well, you *did* ask for a sign!"

He had successfully crossed over. This reception area greeted all manner of things that transcended the realms, from angels and demons to ghosts and psychonauts. Frank Zappa was in one corner having an animated conversation with Timothy Leary. J.C. was still feeling a little wobbly from his journey, and had to brace himself on the arm of the chair. Luckily, the chairs here transfigured themselves into the ideal sitting arrangement for whatever being was resting in them, so it propped him up admirably.

Across the aisle from him, a penguin looked up from a magazine and nodded. Next to it, a statuesque female angel sat in a humanoid form, filing pristine fingernails with a golden file. Several ghostly children chased one another around the room, with a spectral father attempting to shout at them to simmer down, however he had apparently lost the ability to speak in the planar transition, so it just looked like he was practicing a terrible mime act while unable to catch the much faster, younger spirits wreaking havoc in front of him.

J.C. stood, and walked over to a small window formed of clouds and mist. A brass bell sat midair, and he rang it three times. A ball of white light formed behind the window. It was wearing Groucho Marx glasses, to give it some semblance of recognizable facial features. The moustache twitched as a soothing female voice asked: "May I help you?"

"Hello. I hath returned. Please process the paperwork as soon as you can, I am in a hurry."

"Your name?" the ball of light pulsed.

"Jesus."

"I'm sorry, please try again."

J.C. cleared his throat. He then tried to utter his celestial name, a name so impossible to pronounce that even if it were written in ink on paper, it would be thousands of characters long, many of which were letters and characters unfamiliar to anyone in any Earth language.

"I'm sorry, please try again," the light repeated.

"Jesus. Of Nazareth. Jesu? Son of YHWH? Lamb of God? Christ? Master? Shepard? Emmanuel? Chosen one? Bread of life?"

"I'm sorry, but that entity has been assigned to operation second coming, and is not available at this time. Please leave a message and I will ensure that it is received in the order commensurate with the space time continuum."

"Leave a message? No, no, I'm—"

"BEEP," said the ball of light. Its eyebrows wiggled.

Jurassichrist

"I art J.C. I doth not need to leave a message with thee for myself."

The ball glowed a little brighter. "I am sorry you are unhappy with my service. Would you like to hear a joke to lighten the mood? Query: How do you make holy water?

Answer: Boil the hell out of it."

J.C. reached through the window and touched the ball of light. A surge of power electrified his form and shot out through his fingertips. The ball fizzled, the moustache turning to ash and the fake nose and eyebrows exploding from its surface. The ball of light blinked and disappeared, as J.C. climbed through the floating window.

He would apologize for skipping the line later, if someone called him out on it. He hated to play the "I'm YHWH's kid" card, but there was no time to waste with bureaucratic red tape. Time was of the essence.

He found himself in heaven's antechamber, as the waiting room dematerialized behind him. This was a relatively small room, compared to the main chamber colloquially known as heaven, but it was still so vast that the walls weren't even visible from here. J.C. walked through the gate to the golden city with barely a nod to the guard, who looked a bit shocked when he realized who just blew him off.

"Jesus?" the guard floated after J.C. "What are you doing here? I heard you were on assignment for the foreseeable future?"

J.C. kept walking as the guard hovered along beside him, a few inches from the fog-covered floor. They generally kept their plane of existence gravitationally upright, just to help ease the transitions between planes, since most of the through traffic came from places with gravitational pull and other forces of physics. J.C. also found that it allowed him to feel like he was in more of a hurry when he could stamp his feet, instead of softly floating over the ground. "I came back."

"Everything all right?"

"Not really, I—no, don't worry about it, Walter. Everything is fine. I have to go chat with Dad."

"Tell him hello. I haven't seen him around lately. Must be working hard on something."

"I will." J.C. looked back at a long line of angry plane transitioners staring at him. He realized he was acting like a celebrity that was too cool to wait in line with the plebs to get into a hot club, but again, this was urgent. The penguin held up a flipper in what must have been a rude gesture in flightless bird culture and muttered something about "entitled dick," before returning to its magazine.

J.C. allowed the matter around him to shift and willed his atomic structure to materialize in the office of YHWH. The secretary of YHWH sat at a desk made of pure antimatter, doing a multiplicity of office management functions with an uncountable number of limbs. The secretary's multitude of faces all shined with light like he or she was covered in masks that all had high-watt spotlights behind them, shooting visible streams of photons out of the eye and mouth holes. They spoke with the voice of God's will, and even J.C. felt the hairs on the back of his neck stand up when they spoke.

"Good to see you, J.C. I understand that you are currently on Earth circa the twenty-first century. I hope that your second coming is outstanding."

"Hello, Vox. No, I am not on Earth. I am here, before you, and I need to see my father."

"I'm afraid that is impossible, J.C. There are two reasons: One, you are not here, but on Earth in the twenty-first century, as foretold by the prophecies and holy writ. Two, YWYH has indicated that he is not to be disturbed under any circumstances."

"It's me, Vox. Open thine eyes and behold my glory, for I am the Son of God. Now, can you please buzz me in?"

"No can do, J.C. If you are indeed J.C. Which you seem to be, according to all of my senses. Which is also impossible. Because you are in the middle of your second coming. Which is not here, but elsewhere." They opened infinite mouths in multiple layers of reality and grinned. "Now, perhaps I can help you? I speak with the voice of God, after all. Are you concerned because you are in two places at once?"

J.C. paced. "Look, I'm not in two places. I art here. I art here because something has gone horribly wrong. I was sent to the wrong place and time."

"It is impossible for that to have occurred."

"I know. Thus, my concern. Something is horribly wrong."

"If you would like to take a number, I will be happy to page you when YHWH is available?"

"I'm his son. He won't mind if I go in, trust me."

"I cannot allow that. He has forbidden it."

J.C. furrowed his brow. There were so many things wrong with this picture. For one thing, he was still in his human body, thus his ability to do things like brow furrowing and neck hair raising. He should have been transformed back into his energy form and left the shell behind. He pinched his own arm, verifying that it felt squishy.

For another, he was starting to get concerned about his father. YHWH got busy sometimes, but it was rare indeed when he closed his office door to visitors, and even so, Jesus would normally be an exception to any "do not disturb" rule in place. J.C. wondered if something had happened to God. Was that possible? Was Nietzsche right? Had someone found a way to kill God? Furthermore, too many impossible things were happening. One or two impossible things were probably fine, as extra-dimensional beings sometimes trafficked in impossibilities and rewrote reality as needed, but to do so required the kind of power only a few entities could manifest—entities such as the father, the son, the holy ghost, the devil, a few demons, some high level angels, and David Bowie.

What if someone had murdered God?

"I have to get in there," J.C. said, walking toward the door.

"Sir, I must ask you to stop, I have been ordered to stop anyone from disturbing the lord, and I will use force if I must." They stretched out a hand and a forcefield of golden light formed a wall in front of J.C. For a moment, the son of man concentrated, and then he parted his hands, severing the wall and ripping a hole in the forcefield.

The voice of God stood and reached a million arms toward J.C., grabbing his lanky body and holding him fast. J.C. turned his steely gaze upon the super-angel and blasted them with eye lasers, forcing them to let go with a cry of agony. "I am the prince of peace, but I know how to make war! Dad has given me authority to execute judgment, because I am the Son of Man. Now, stand down!"

J.C. kicked the massive celestial door. If his father was in trouble, he might be the only one able to save him. He leaped through the portal with a battle cry.

Nothing seemed different, except there was no God in this room.

A gigantic, horrific creature of pure chaos

turned and fixed countless eyes upon him, roaring and waving tentacles about as it gibbered like something out of a nightmare.

Book 14

J.C. screamed and leapt forward, rolling into a combat-ready position. As he moved, he summoned his massive gun. He wanted a weapon that he was at least somewhat familiar with. As he exited his roll, he braced himself and fired on the tentacled monstrosity before him. Bullets tore through the creature, but the barrage did not seem to slow it down as it charged forward, smashing ethereal furniture and leaving a trail of devastation behind it.

A massive orange tentacle swung toward him. J.C. leapt at the last possible moment, rolling over it to the floor like a car crash victim over the windshield of a Buick. As he picked himself up off the floor, something hit him from behind, and he sprawled forward. The shambling eyesore was holding him down with two tentacles, and it deftly flipped him on his back, gibbering madly with multiple mouths.

The monster looked surprised when it saw that the flipped-over J.C. was now holding a grenade. "Suck on this, thee blasphemy against order!" He fired it upward from the gut, and the grenade exploded mid-air just below the monster's gaping maw. The concussive force was enough to separate the two combatants. Smoke and flame engulfed everything, and J.C. was suddenly in the middle of a hurricane of pain. Fragments of unidentifiable substances peppered his skin, and he felt multiple wounds spray a variety of liquids out of his broken body.

J.C. was in the corner of the room now. He groaned, turning on his side. It had been a risky move, blowing himself up, but he would regenerate. He only hoped that it had done as much or more damage to the eldritch horror.

He was a bloody mess. His flesh began to knit itself together, the holes closing up and the blood flow staunching. Once his knees could function again, he pulled himself up into a crawling position and peered through the smoke. The creature was invisible through the cloud, but J.C. could hear it breathing and making wet sucking noises.

A huge tentacle erupted forth from the smoke and caught J.C. in the chest, slamming him backward and flinging him through the door through which he'd entered. The multi-faced voice of God still sat at their desk, working on some kind of celestial spreadsheets and filing infinite nails.

J.C. reached up and popped his jaw back into place. He could feel the cartilage growing back together, and held it still as he tried to say, "Help!" through a mostly broken face. "Theresh a monshter in theresh and itsh trying to deshtroy God and hish universh! Help me kill it!"

Their most apologetic faces pointed toward J.C. "I'm sorry, but YHWH said he did not wish to be disturbed. If I assisted you in having an epic, over-the-top battle in his inner sanctum, that would be disturbing indeed."

"You can't dishturb him if hesh not—" J.C. forgot his aching jaw temporarily, as another tentacle came swinging out the door, wrapped itself around his waist, and pulled him back into his dad's office. The smoke had cleared a bit, revealing the space to be pretty wrecked.

The gibbering thing had chunks missing and was spitting an opaque, milky fluid out of multiple spouts and nodules on its body. It brought him up close to its many mouths, jabbering in archaic, untranslatable languages.

"Die, swine! Thou hath not bested me yet!" Reaching deep inside for supernatural strength, J.C. tore his arms free of the tentacle's sticky and powerful grip. He wound up for a right cross, and punched the burbling horror directly in the face. The blow landed exactly where the creature's nose would be, had it a nose. It's many eyes closed in pain, as it winced backward.

"AaaaAAAAAAArrrrgggghhhhssssstop it!" The tentacle dropped J.C. who landed on his feet, and swung his gun around to fire some more rounds. He was glad he opted to summon the shoulder strap, otherwise he'd have been disarmed by the explosion. He was also lucky that at least one of his shoulders had been relatively unbroken by the blast.

The gun roared to life, firing round after round point blank into the monster's many eyes. J.C. screamed his battle cry as hot shells littered the ground around them. "Eat lead, demon!"

The horror roared in frustration. "Sssssstop it! Stop it, Jesus! Cut it out!" There was a massive flash of light and the smell of petrichor, as though a long rain had just ended and the first rainbow was emerging from the gloom. The creature was rapidly transforming, growing smaller as its limbs and appendages folded in on themselves. It was like watching space collapse on itself, and any mortal would have gone insane, watching the non-euclidean geometry defy the laws of physics.

Matter cannot be created or destroyed, only changed. That's a fine rule, when you're in the mortal realm, but when you're in a plane beyond time and space and able to complete impossible tasks, it works more similarly to brewing beer. Just how most states permit homebrewing of 100 gallons of beer per adult per year, most of the higher planes in the multiverse permit the creation or destruction of up to twelve billion base units, depending, of course, on the atomic weight or molecular weight divided by the molar mass constant.

"Dad?"

YHWH stood before his son, dusting himself off. His normally pristine robes were tattered and grey, covered in mysterious stains. "Jesus

Jurassichrist

Christ! And, I mean that in the pejorative sense, not in the nomenclatural." The creator of the universe yelled into the antechamber. "Vox, I thought I told you that I didn't want to be disturbed!"

The voice of God echoed back, the loudest thing in the multiverse: "That's what I told him."

"Well, why didn't you stop him?"

The voice responded: "He is Jesus, and Jesus cannot be here, therefore there was nobody to stop."

God muttered under his breath and waved his arms, repairing and remaking his throne room-cum-office. "Everyone here is so literal. I hate it." He slumped into his office chair, which was the great golden throne of God foretold of in legend, only he had added castors so he could wheel around the room and spin in place.

"Father? That . . . that abomination was . . . ?"

God shrugged. "All right, we need to talk. Have a seat."

There were no chairs. J.C. formed a puffy beanbag-chair-looking cloud of mist and plopped himself down in it. "I thought you were hurt. What was that thing?"

"That thing, as you put it, was, well . . . me."

Michael Allen Rose

J.C.'s father had changed forms before, but never into something that truly terrifying and alien. Other deities were well known for such tricks. Zeus liked to change into animals to seduce and fuck random humans. Anansi got a kick out of running around as a spider. Hell, one time, during a celestial game of truth or dare, Hades had dared Loki to disguise himself as an automatic teller machine in Los Angeles, California in the late 1990s and the son-of-a-gun had raised about $500 for a charity that made toupees for turtles. This was straight-up Lovecraftian elder-God shit, though—and that was unusual, to say the least, especially for the so-called "Judeo-Christian God."

"Why would you change into—?" J.C. asked.

"Into that? I didn't change into that. I am that. That is me, baby boy." YHWH threw his hands up and unfolded space, his matter rearranging itself before J.C.'s very eyes. Before long, God had transformed back into the monster and was tapping a tentacle on his desk. He opened a drawer and removed a sparkling bag of glowing powder, which he poured out onto the desk, and using the tip of his appendage, cut it into lines. A butthole-like orifice opened up like the mouth of a lamprey and sucked the powder away. "Whooo! Oh yes," he barked, throwing his gelatinous head backward and allowing his eyes to beam out waves of color. "Angel dust. Real shit, from actual angels. You want a little toot-toot? Keeps you sharp." J.C. let his open-hanging jaw decline for him, and tried to look composed. God continued: "It's more difficult to make human syllables in this form—my true form, by the way—but maybe this will all make more sense to you if we talk face to faces instead of hiding behind the mug of a human. It was really a silly bet with that fucko Cthulhu that started it."

"This cannot be your physical form, Father. The Bible says that you created man in your own image. This image!" J.C. gestured to himself, stepping closer to the thing.

"The Bible was written by MEN, not me, my man-child. They needed something to hold on to. I went along with it. Fine. I'll pretend I look like a hairless ape. Can you imagine the headache if I showed up like this? They'd shit coconuts." The thing gibbered from several mouths at once.

"I don't understand."

"J.C., my baby boy, you need to level up. Get

a clue. That place down there? That's not the real world. I mean, it is, but this, up here, this is the really real world. I honestly hoped you would never see me like this. I suppose I should come clean. Man was not created in the image of God. Man is an aberration that should have been erased, but my pride wouldn't let me relay that information to you, J.C. The whole thing is quite embarrassing."

"An aberration? But you love them . . . "

"Woah, woah, woah, let's not use words we don't mean. Love? No, I mean . . . I set things up to generally make their lives pleasant enough the first time around, but humans were created as a slave race. I needed something that wouldn't fight back, that would do my bidding, feed my ego, and build some monuments to me. Humans were the result of a carefully planned, billion year evolutionary cycle. You sure you don't want a bump?"

J.C. stared. "Father, you said the first time around. What do you mean, first?"

The thing called God looked sheepish and turned, shuffling back behind his massive desk. "This time, things will go better. I'm tweaking the formula."

"This time around?"

Jurassichrist

"Aren't you supposed to be doing your second coming?"

"That's just it. It did not work. Thine own son was sent to a far flung past, devoid of humans. Which you seem to think of as nothing more than cannon fodder. Can this be true? Father, why have you forsaken them?" J.C. was confused and angry. This was unexpected and almost too terrible to contemplate. Mankind, the very creature his own form was based on, meant to be a race of slaves?

"Look, J.C., take some time off. Your mission failed, and that's okay. I have plenty of backup plans. This time, evolution will work out. I've run the scenarios, and this is the best way forward. Why don't you go down to the beach and eat some cosmic ice cream?"

J.C. stared blankly, as the gears turned in his head. "You're forcing evolution. It was you." Of course it was God. Who else could supply the kind of magic and transgress the line of impossibility to give the mammals their products as seen on tee vee?

J.C. stalked toward his father, but the deity held out a hand of pure light and stopped the son in his tracks. "Son, don't do this. Just walk away." The wall of light kept J.C. from advancing, despite his holy powers.

"Father . . . answer me one question. Why didst thou keep the truth of the dinosaurs from me? Why hide their glory?"

The light dimmed and God lowered his defenses, scowling. "Dinosaurs. That was my biggest mistake, allowing them to flourish. Peace, love, and harmony are all just fine, when you're not trying to run a universe. Democracy is a joke. Mortal creatures need a leader. They need guidelines. They need to be afraid. Those bird lizards got too big too fast and didn't need me. They have their blasted humming."

J.C. was pushing ever closer, feeling YHWH's concentration falter as he was distracted, thinking of his great folly. "They didn't need thee? So . . . thou . . . is that why the era ended with destruction?"

"They had to go extinct. Their ability to control the forces of the universe through will, using the hum, refining materials meant for the gods, they didn't need me." God waved a hand and a slideshow appeared in mid-air behind him. It showed pictures of mammals, rutting, excreting, being filthy, low and base. "Now these creatures . . . they need me, kiddo. They can't handle the universe without their God. And this time, evolution two-point-oh, they'll fall into line even deeper. After the extinction event, they'll learn everything I want them to from tee-vee. Their society will be dependent on technology before the first humans ever develop. Mammal society will have an extra hundred million years to develop into the pathetic, needy creatures that I want them to be. They'll never abandon me."

God reached into his desk and pulled forth a jet black cross, smooth and shiny and glowing with an eerie purple shimmer, like a bowling ball under a blacklight.

"That's a stave of evolution." J.C. recognized it immediately. It was one of the tools the architects had used to create the universe and everything in it. He had wielded them himself on numerous occasions, when working on large subjects and concepts like "water," "dirt" and "heat," and even relatively smaller projects like "a zebra's digestive system." Except this one wasn't golden.

"I have changed it with my touch. This one is so charged that it will exceed even the most stringent factors of impossibility. It's a reset button, my son."

"Father, it is corrupted."

"Whatever you want to call it, kid. Listen, I

didn't want you to see behind the curtain. That's why I sent you away. I figured you'd just hang out in the Mesozoic era until all this was over, come back here, and your whole mortal history would be erased. You'd be just another spirit, no need to sacrifice yourself for ungrateful mortals and go through all that table-flipping in temples and wandering in deserts. Just kick back by heaven's pool and snort some angel dust. Let me handle everything."

"But without my sacrifice, how would they be rewarded in the afterlife?"

"They wouldn't. They'd rot. But that doesn't affect you or I." God had his omniscience, but he was obviously concentrating it elsewhere as J.C. had forced his way into God's immediate vicinity, without being noticed. The deity still babbling about his need for subservience. With a sudden burst a speed, he reached out and grabbed hold of God's tentacle, pulling the black cross from his grasp.

"I will not allow you to destroy the dinosaurs for the sake of your own ego."

YHWH roared angrily and belched a mess of black bile out of his many gibbering facial orifices. J.C. backed away and headed for the door, black cross in tow. "Give it back, you rebellious little shit!"

"Nay, Father, thou shalt not fuck with my people!" J.C. ran, as huge sharp clouds of spikes stabbed through heaven's floor around him. He heard the angry rage of his father shaking the walls of the entire plane of existence, as he sprinted past the voice of God.

"Have a nice day!" said the voice, waving one of their many hands.

A moment later, a black cloud of violence rolled forth from God's office, a storm a hundred yards high and fronted with a countenance of pure hate.

"GIVE ME MY CROSS!" the thunder roared.

J.C. put as much distance between himself and the creator of the universe as he could, leaping over spontaneously manifesting obstacles and running right past Walter, the guard, who just blinked and lowered his newspaper. He was about to say something when the black cloud rolled over him, the golden gates, and everything, with a scream that shattered the heavens.

J.C. put everything else on hold, even his own healing body, still aching from the frag grenade, and concentrated. Using all the power

Michael Allen Rose

left within him, he blasted himself sideways across dimensions, his material essence transforming. The cloud rolled on toward him, reaching out tendrils of black hate, unhampered by time or space, existing simultaneously everywhere and always. Just before the cloud devoured him, J.C. felt his spirit transcend heaven and slam forcefully into full on mortality, and disappeared from the metaverse. He clung tightly to the black cross, feeling waves of pure power emanating from within. The dark tendrils closed on empty air, and all of heaven shook with the rage of YHWH.

J.C. was on his way back. As he sped through space and time, targeting the jungles of the Cenozoic, he thought about how he had to save his people from a mad god. But which ones were "his people?" In a truly just world, it seemed that the dinosaurs were doing far more to uphold the dignity and morality that J.C. had always professed to hold dear, but the mammals were his genetic ancestors. He had some difficult time and bad memories associated with his time on Earth, but he had also had a rich, full life, talking philosophy, fishing with his friends, and finding love with

Jurassichrist

the beautiful Mary Magdalene. Those experiences had shaped who he was today, so how could he discount them and let them fade into nonexistence? Far below him, stood the familiar volcano, and he willed his form speeding toward it. Until recently, he'd have said that he was the son of god and man. But now, he wasn't so sure.

Book 15

J.C. slammed into the center of the volcano, plunging deep beneath the lava, and was immediately incinerated. This was an unforeseen problem.

The melted savior was atomized into his component parts, a billion atoms changing form to become part of the rock, the endless flow of fire and ash. His plunge into the liquid rock was witnessed only by Eoraptor, who happened to be stargazing at the time.

Eoraptor sighed heavily. He picked up the golden cross that he had found so long ago and began his trek down the mountain. It took him some time to get to the base of it, being older than most rocks and some dirt, and with the weather as it was, his arthritic knees weren't helping either. Finally, he entered the golden city, a place he had watched from the time it had first been constructed, through the ages, as dinosaurs learned to harness the hum and commune with the elements, and up to this most recent turn of events. He did not like to visit the city, preferring instead to while away his time researching and meditating, studying his little piece of celestial magic, and writing erotic fan fiction. He had been chiseling a particularly spicy tale about three atomic particles and a single-celled organism that were all into BDSM, and was just getting to the fusion part of the story. This moment in history, however, was too important to waste. The cross had told him so, in one of his many visions.

When J.C. had first showed up, Eoraptor couldn't be certain. Hallucinations and dementia affected even the immortal. But, once he had heard the human speak, he knew. This golden bit of creation belonged to the human, and with that knowledge came the responsibility of helping make things right when the time came.

"The time is now!" he mind-blasted to all the dinosaurs in the Wrap.

Myron met him at the door. "Eoraptor?"

"Gather all your top dinosaurs together. Generals, intellectuals, anyone you think would be useful in an Apocalypse scenario. We're going to need some food, water, supplies, and most importantly, something to do." Eoraptor let himself in, pushing past the confused ceratops.

"Something to do?" Myron asked, puzzled.

"We're going to be waiting a while."

Meanwhile, inside the bowels of the Earth:

The flesh that was once Jesus Christ of Nazareth, Yehoshua, The Lamb of God, the holy made flesh, Christus the Anointed One, that guy in the paintings with the long hair and blue eyes who is really a middle-eastern fellow but middle America can't admit it because it flies in the face of their societal institutional racism, Doctor J, and Jebus had been physically reduced to nothing but ash, flue gas, and heat. He was so deep inside the magma that he couldn't leak out by conduction, no matter how hard he jiggled the thermal energy that was still, technically, him. After attempting the gradual transmission of energy from the Earth's mantle up to the crust for about a thousand years or so, J.C. got very tired. He allowed his kinetic energy to, at last, transform into pure thermal energy, and floated about for a few millennia, riding the tectonic plates, surfing the nether regions of the world while the continents cracked and grinded. His spirit sank and contracted until it inhabited one single atom of calcium.

Jesus remained a calcium atom for a few more millennia, until he gathered together with other atoms of a similar nature. As one of the only sentient atoms he was aware of, it was difficult to cope with the crushing boredom of being an atom. Now that he had found a group of similar individuals, he felt a little more like himself. In fact, the more he jiggled and interacted with them, the further down the road toward cohesion he travelled, until one day he formed some chemical bonds and became a molecule.

The molecule that contained J.C.'s essence floated around a while longer, and one day, he realized that he was no longer part of a lava flow, but had, at some point, become part of a calcified deposit in some limestone. This was a refreshing change, and J.C. enjoyed the porous new scenery, until once again, he became bored with the still and placid life of molecular living, and thoughts of his current situation crept in.

Michael Allen Rose

The dripping cave water running over his limestone home felt cool. He remembered things being hot, and then later, cool. He remembered feeling things and saving people. He remembered the dinosaurs and he remembered his fight with his father. Then, he began to recall how he had arrived here. What had happened to the black cross, after he was obliterated? What of his friends? Where, and when, was he?

His senses, honed beyond those of normal mortal matter, reached out, searching for signs of life, changes in the environment, any information that would allow his mind to make the connections that he was looking for. Like the whiskers of a cat, his consciousness expanded, feeling around for stimulus.

A vibration of sound waves resonated, and only his past experience as a sentient being ensured his ability to decode it as a voice.

"You poked me."

J.C. expanded his consciousness once again, adding the ability to see and communicate to his already stalwart arsenal of tactile and audible sensations.

"Excuse me?" asked J.C., of the calcium carbonate compound.

"I was poked."

The thing had a long, plump body and a scrunched-up head. It stood on eight legs, each ending in four tiny clawed hands.

"I'm sorry for poking you. What are you?"

The microscopic creature writhed around, apparently thinking this over. "I'm not sure. What are you?"

J.C. tried to answer this, but was stumped. "I think I'm a man, but I think I'm a god, too. I might be part of a rock. I was in a volcano, so I think I might have been fire too."

"I was in a volcano, too!" said the tiny creature, wiggling its arms happily.

"Really? How are you still alive?"

The creature wrinkled its face into something like a smile. "I survived by going into an almost death-like state I invented. I call it cryptobiosis. You see, I curl into a dehydrated ball by retracting my head and legs. Then I take a nap until I am reintroduced to water. After that, I can come back to life in just a few hours."

"So, something introduced you to water?"

"The drops come from above. I think you and your rock moved. Now there are drippings."

Talking to this little creature connected errant synapses and nodes in the meta-mind of the molecule who was once a god, and he expanded his consciousness further still. "You're a tardigrade!"

"Am I?" said the tardigrade, swimming forward in the trickle of water and grabbing a piece of lichen between its sharp little teeth. "That's great. Are you a tardigrade, too?"

J.C. began to remember. "No, I was a man and a god and a rock and all those things, but it was all because of a terrible accident. I burned up and forgot, for a time."

"You burned up? You should try being fireproof."

"You're right," J.C. chuckled.

"I like you, god man rock fire thing. You are nice to . . . Tardigrade?"

"Yes," J.C. said to the gentle creature. "Tardigrade."

This creature was so innocent, so helpful, so unlike the warlike, so called *higher* life forms he had interacted with. Love burned inside J.C.'s core, his electrons speeding around his nuclei, and everything fell into place. He felt love for this tiny tardigrade, and that love reminded him of the larger, more expansive love he had felt for the human race. Then, he recalled the love for the dinosaurs, for the birds, for all the creations he'd invested so much in. Then, there was the betrayal of his father, the corruption of love and the sick and twisted desire for power and control that had led to this.

"Tardigrade, thou hast helped bring me back from the void. Thou shall be blessed among all creatures."

"I shall?" replied the tardigrade, mouth filled with delicious moss.

J.C. had saved up a ridiculous amount of holy power, having not used any of his magic for so very long. He summoned his power, growing in intensity, pulling other atoms into his aura and re-building his body from the component parts of the universe.

"Yes. For all eternity, thou shalt survive all cosmic events, even those that would cause the extinction of other creatures. Earth-pummeling asteroids, nearby supernova blasts and gamma-ray bursts shall be as water over your back. Huge numbers of species, or even an entire genus may become extinct, but life as a whole will go on, in thee."

"Gee, thanks, you're a peach!" said the tardigrade, swimming off. "See you later!"

The holy magic was bursting out of him,

now, growing in intensity by the second. J.C.
felt good, knowing that no matter what
happened with his war against his father's evil
plan, he would always have tardigrades.

Without a stave, controlling this amount of
energy was immensely taxing, hurting his mind
like an icepick to the cerebrum. Slowly,
painfully, his familiar human body formed. He
felt the water from above splashing across skin
instead of mineral, and he twitched his fingers
and toes, making sure that they worked after
such a long non-existence. His long-denied
mission came into clear focus, and he breathed
in for the first time in an epoch.

The air tasted funny. He leaned back to
cough, and water poured down his throat.

Sputtering, he opened his eyes to see that he
was in a cave, underneath a constantly dripping
waterfall that had naturally broken through the
rock above. This had once been a volcano, and
apparently, millions of years later, lay dormant.

He moved out from under the pouring water
and summoned a flame for light. The cave was
small and dark. A large rock had fallen and
rolled into the passage to close it off, long ago.

"Jesus strength, go!" Buffing his muscles
with holy magic, he pushed the boulder. At

first, it was futile, but finally, with great effort, he began to roll it. Just like he did during his famous escape from the tomb post-resurrection, J.C. heaved with one final massive effort. The surface soil cracked and crumbled as the boulder emerged from the mountainside and crashed down the side of the peak on which he stood, looking over the land.

A rumble above him indicated that he needed to move. J.C. ran down the hill, just in time to avoid another cave-in from the ridge above, which quickly filled in and covered over the cave from which he had emerged with mounds of rock and snow. He carefully found his footing, trying not to cause any more landslides in this arid terrain.

It was now sixty-six million years before the first coming, and several dozen-million years after his second, and things were notably different. Glaciers slid around on the horizon, slowly flattening a path across the dividing continents. The air was sooty and filtered the sunlight to a reddish haze. J.C. looked across the icy devastation, struggling to breathe in the atmosphere of nuclear winter. Based on the amount of soot in the global debris layer above, J.C. could only assume that the entire terrestrial biosphere had burned, implying a global soot-cloud blocking out the sun. How long ago?

Extinction events or not, he had to get off this mountain. He had spent eons as heat, and it would be too ironic to freeze to death now. J.C. had no idea what direction to go, or where to find life. Then, as the sun broke through a cloud of gray, a mote of gleaming light sparked across the desolate land, down in the valley. It looked like the ruins of what might have been a small structure of some kind in the very distant past, tarnished, but still somehow shining just enough to serve as a beacon.

Shivering, he made his way carefully down the steep face of the mountain to uncover what mysteries might lay in the ruins below.

Book 16

This was the strangest thing J.C. had ever seen, and that was saying a lot. It was like the oricalchum that he'd found during his second coming, but dull, and robbed of its magical properties. Once he had cleared away the layer of frost, he found smooth metal. It was only a patch, a small cube thrusting up from beneath the ground. It was strangely warmer than the surrounding Earth, though the heat was weak, as if it was hooked to some kind of generator that could only be on the lowest of standby power.

J.C. poked at it, and tapped it. It was a solid piece, and looked like it had been buried for thousands of years, perhaps longer. It was surprisingly not oxidized or rusted, and stood out like a sore thumb against the dead white plains around him.

It became clear: this mountain was the site of the great dinosaur city. He was looking at what amounted to a fossil, a dead memory of his friends and it was only then, finally, that true desolation sunk into his soul.

He had failed. He failed the dinosaurs, the humans, and the planet. The great extinction event had come, and he missed it, so his second coming had been for naught, his third coming saw him alone in this ice age, and there would be no fourth.

For miles around where he stood, there was only empty nature. Where the great city had stood, there was stone and soil, its road long since decayed into dust and taken back by the creeping vines and hardy weeds that were able to survive with the diminished sunlight in this age of ruin.

Once again, he touched the surface of the metal. It was obviously oricalchum, perhaps serving as a capstone atop an ancient skyscraper. It was impossible to tell whether the city was completely destroyed through the ravages of time, or at least partially still here, but buried.

He had an eternity to find out. He decided to dig. At first, with his hands, then, after resting a bit, he found that his power had returned to the level he needed to summon up a shovel, and soon he had dug out the sides of the cube another foot or two. He brushed the sides, and noticed that the temperature, once tepid, had increased to a steady heat.

J.C. continued to excavate, and after a short while, he had unearthed a small, hinged piece on the side of the cube. It looked as if it had been designed to protect something. With some difficulty, he worked the grit-encrusted hinges and flipped the protective lid open. Underneath, there was some sort of glass, marbled with streaks of blue ichor. As soon as it was exposed to the light, it sparkled with pinpoints of sapphire beauty, the sunlight forming a beam inside the glass and focusing the photons somewhere downward of his position.

After a few moments, there was a rumble from below. At first, J.C. thought perhaps he had somehow triggered an earthquake or some other seismic activity, the volcano behind him looming large in his mind. Then, the rumble stopped and he heard a small, strangely familiar voice bubble up from the earth. It sounded a bit muffled, like it was coming from somewhere far away.

"Squeee honk barrrrk roarrrp grrrwwwofff."

J.C. frowned. "What?"

"It spoke." A rustle of activity. The sound of things moving around. The clearing of a throat. "Put your face to the window."

The only window was the glass that he had revealed with his investigation. He leaned over, carefully, and put his face up to it, trying to see inside.

"Back up!"

"Excuse me?" J.C. said, confused.

"You're blocking all the light. Back up!"

J.C. crawled backwards, holding his robe above the dirt. The beam of light, unblocked, travelled down the strange tube once again. "I'm sorry? Who is—"

"It's him! It's him! Roooooaaar! Gronk! Gronk! Gronk! Rawwwwwk!"

There was a huge commotion, like a shopping cart filled with pots and pans had careened down a flight of stairs, and then the strange signal went silent.

"Hello? Is anyone there?" J.C. cried, pawing at the glass, but no answer came. He stood up, unsure of what to do.

Jurassichrist

The air was chilly and J.C. shivered in his robes. It had taken an immense amount of power to regenerate from near nothingness, but as soon as his power had replenished somewhat, summoning a nice down jacket and maybe some snow pants was on his short list of things to do.

It startled him when a warm wind blew, supplying a moment of comfort in this frosty climate. He turned toward the source of the heat and, to his astonishment, the ground cracked open. A horizontal line, splitting the surface of the ground stretched further apart until a blue light shone out from beneath the ground. It was as though the Earth itself was building stairs, starting with the ground floor.

As the snow and soil fell, it became clear that the line ended after about ten fathoms. It was a hatch of some kind, cut and designed and installed here for some inscrutable purpose. Whatever mechanisms were at work struggled against the weight of burial, grinding and hissing with the change in pressure between the surface and whatever lay below.

Against a backdrop of cerulean light came shadows, silhouettes rising up from the subterranean void. First, a ridged circle, like a giant cabbage, then beside that a much larger oval that clearly was the head of some massive serpent. Finally, a smaller body leaped up from under the rapidly opening portal, walking two legged and waving its arms frantically.

"J.C., it's you! Come, quickly, inside!"

Myron, the ridged ceratops, the primordial Eoraptor, and the huge head of General Arius all smiled large toothy grins at him.

"How . . . how is this possible? How dost thou know me? I have been dead for a million years or more. Thou canst not be alive, still!"

Myron slowly crawled up out of the hatch and placed a large, meaty arm on the shoulder of J.C., carefully bringing the human toward the mysterious doorway. "Come, we will explain all, but we must hurry inside, before—"

"Before what?" J.C. asked, but the dinosaurs had all stopped speaking, and were listening, ears pricked up. Just like birds, of which dinosaurs are a kind, dinos do not have visible external ears, so it is very difficult indeed to "prick them up." It would be like a human trying to "prick up" a nostril to smell something further away. But these dinosaurs were nothing if not ambitious, and judging from their facial expressions, terribly concerned.

Jurassichrist

General Arius growled. In his lowest voice, which was still frighteningly loud, he grumbled, "Get inside. Now, human."

J.C. walked toward the hatch. "How is it that thou speakest my language? The last time we met, we had to use our minds to—"

"We had a lot of time to practice. Now, please, hurry," said Myron, ushering J.C. forward with haste.

A single, blood-curdling howl rose up in the air from somewhere above. It was quickly joined, as a chorus of loud, doleful cries broke the stillness.

"They have the high ground! Run!" Eoraptor belched, skittering past Myron and J.C. and diving headfirst into the bunker.

"Close it, General!" Myron shouted, as he and J.C. reached the opening. The hatch began to grind downward, sputtering and catching on bits of rock and soil. All three dinosaurs started humming, and the machinery picked up a little speed.

A pack of creatures appeared, converging from the surrounding hills and heading straight for the little group. They looked like a cross between wolves and tigers, large, hairy and filled with teeth. They were armored up in "As

Seen On TV" items, paws outfitted with Pet Deshedding Gloves for traction, bodies covered in ballistic armor made from screen protectors and coated with a combination of Pink Armor Nail Gel and Diamond Armor window treatments, and loaded up with weapons ranging from the Stun N' Run TASER to mace to batons that could be extended with the flick of a wrist.

They were smaller than the dinosaurs—much smaller than the General—but the technology and their vicious savagery, not to mention the numbers game, made them a potentially fatal threat. It appeared that the mammals had absolutely flourished in the time since J.C.'s aborted second coming, and evolved to be more dangerous, cunning, and savage than ever before.

"Kill! Kill! Kill!" the pack screamed as they descended upon the slowly closing door.

"Ahhhhhhh!" J.C. screamed, as the terrifying mammals grew close enough to show the blackness in their focused eyes and the white of their canine teeth as they leaped forward, sensing easy prey.

The hatch door finally closed, just in the nick of time. Three loud thumps rang through the metal, as Myron reached up and secured several metal bars across the hatch. He breathed deeply and sighed, sliding his back down and crashing to the ground, exhausted and relieved.

"It's good to see you, my boy," said Eoraptor, gesturing for J.C. to follow. "We were starting to think maybe you'd never come back."

J.C. followed, with the other dinosaurs close behind. The General did his best not to step on any part of J.C. in the relatively cramped quarters. They were heading down a hallway, which descended until it came to a branching passage. They kept walking through the central corridor. Everything was dull, and brassy, a far cry from the glorious shine of the oricalchum that he had witnessed the last time he was here. It took him a few minutes to even recognize that he was indeed in what had once been "The Wrap." Once they reached the central room, it was unmistakable. The central dais once held impressive holograms and strategic meetings. Now, there were only a few dinosaurs, and it was no longer the bustling hub of activity it had once been. Everyone was now grim and resolute, with a slight air of madness about them, the kind that comes from long periods of time in solitude.

"I'm sure you have questions," Eoraptor said, falling into a resting slump against a chair. The chairs no longer had the elasticity they had previously exhibited, now sculpted into a variety of abstract and obnoxious shapes that could barely be called furniture. It was obvious from the way Eoraptor squirmed, as he tried to get comfortable, that the once magical devices were now only marginally better than sitting on the floor. The whole room looked dismal, fallen from grace. The only new and shiny looking thing in the room, in fact, was in the center of the pedestal formerly used as a screen. It was the golden stave of creation, propped upright in a place of reverence.

"That I do," J.C. said, as a nearby, tired looking Compsognathus brought him a cup of water, shakily holding it in a trembling claw not designed for such things. He sipped it as he waved the dinos on. "Please, though, tell me, how are you still alive? What happened here? How did you know I would find you?"

"We didn't. All we had was hope," said Myron, sadly.

Eoraptor creakily climbed up on the central table, which was the size of about ten of J.C.'s carpentry benches. Touching the stave of creation with reverence, he turned to J.C. "I had this thing a long time, and after you left, I waited and watched. What must have felt like a few lifetimes to you, up in the other place, felt like only a day or so to us. I was watching the night sky when you reappeared, and as soon as I saw you land, I knew we were in for a rough time." As J.C. jumped up and pulled himself into one of the oversized dinosaur chairs, Eoraptor began to act out the past few millennia with his claws, as a sort of weird, makeshift puppet show.

When Jesus splashed into the volcano and been obliterated, Eoraptor had made a decision. Knowing that the cross, this strange stave from another time, had extended his life far beyond the realm of impossibility, he took it from its place and brought it to the city of the dinosaurs. Once he explained what had happened to Myron and the others, they decided upon a conspiracy that was strikingly bold but necessary to ensure the future of their present. They had constructed this bunker, in the heart of the Wrap, and sworn to secrecy, they lived like a ruling council in secret from then on. They were forced to watch as their society advanced, then receded, and then finally, the end they knew would come did so. Thanks to the visions from the golden cross, this small band of dinosaurs was able to hide from the apocalypse.

It took only a few days from the time it was first spotted in the sky for the meteor to impact. When it did so, it was with the force of a hundred nuclear bombs, making a crater over one-hundred and eighty kilometers wide and absolutely wreaking havoc on the ecosystem. Plants dried up as the sun was blocked by rising ash. The climate changed. The impact zone itself had decimated dinosaur society, taking out several major cities and some important sources of their ichor and oricalchum.

Still, they waited in their bunker, hoping that they could set it all right when J.C. came back for attempt number three.

They watched as the mammals grew and changed, remaining in their stinking tunnels only long enough to weather the storm and adapt to the changing environment, then striking out, growing, becoming more bold and aggressive. During the past few million years, mammals had become the dominant kingdom on the planet, and with the steady influx of As Seen On TV products, as supplied by YHWH above, they rapidly became too powerful to curb. The mammals were slaves to the magic box, which supplied them with a steady and constant stream of information and propaganda, straight from the creator.

The dinosaurs were extinct. Except here, in this little room under the ground.

"So, that cube was a message for me? A beacon, thou hast left?" J.C. asked.

"Yes," explained Eoraptor. "We have had to maintain what little power we have through the hum and concentrate it on keeping that cube above ground, warm enough to melt through the ice and protected so that some fateful day, when you came back to help us, you would find us and know that all is not lost."

"But things may be lost, indeed. My father . . . he . . . he is the one who helps the mammals even now to dominate the Earth. His plan is to redesign the humans . . . make them his personal servants, an army that mindlessly does his bidding. He has all the power in the universe, there is no way to stop him." J.C. hung his head in despair.

The room filled with silence until, finally, General Arius puffed his enormous chest and spoke with authority. "Surely you won't let some deity win without fighting back? Were you not part of the process by which all this was made? We built the most advanced society in the history of creation, once, and with your power assisting us, surely we can take back the Earth from this scourge."

"By the time they evolve into humans, they will be so corrupt and so powerful, no other species will be able to survive. They will kill this planet in the name of God."

Myron thought for a moment. "Aren't you part of this God thing, yourself? The part that is not corrupt?"

"Corrupt." That struck a chord. J.C. suddenly remembered the black cross. Perhaps there was a way, after all. "I stole the tool he was using to remake creation. I brought it here, to keep it from him."

Eoraptor chirped excitedly. "Where is this tool now?"

J.C. looked up. "It was lost, in the volcano."

The General snarled with determination. "Well then . . . we'll simply have to go find it."

Book 17

It was the dead of night when J.C., Myron, and Eoraptor carefully raised the hatch, under the watchful eye of General Arius.

"I'm coming with you. You need protection. What if you're attacked by those putrid things? They'll rip you to pieces." The General snorted.

"You won't fit into the tunnels, General. We've tried." Myron shook his head, his large bony ceratops ruffle the only scaled part of him remaining. He and Eoraptor had shed their scale suits, and were now fully feathered. "We need to be as lithe and agile as possible to navigate those caves."

"I'm aware of that," said General Arius, climbing out of the bunker and nodding at a smaller Hadrosaur, who began the closing process behind the group. "But you have to make it there first. It won't matter, getting through the tunnels, if you're slaughtered before you get there."

J.C. noted that all three dinos wore additional feathers around their feet, a method by which they hoped to increase their stealth. The General, however, still wore his scales, and had apparently changed for battle. The Spinosaur had a row of six-foot-long spines thrusting out of his back like a phalanx of spears, and his twenty-ton body was covered in armor-like studded scales. His teeth shone in the moonlight, a garden of death.

The night was eerily silent now, only the gentle rustling of ferns breaking the quiet. The pack of mammals had long since abandoned the area, or so it seemed.

"Do they know where you live?" J.C. asked.

Myron glanced at his human companion. "We don't believe they know much about us at all. It's ironic, really. Over the past epoch, we have swapped situations in many ways. The mammals, previously hiding underground in their lairs, have become a dominant kingdom and most of them live unfettered out in the open now—whereas we, who once founded cities and roamed the land, have been exiled to the tunnels below.

"And thou hast been living beneath the Earth all this time?"

"Correct. For a very long time, we have only been venturing out when absolutely necessary. The stave of creation that Eoraptor has in his possession keeps us from aging or injury, as long as we remain close to it," said Myron.

"Which is why we need to make this mission a short one," Eoraptor chimed in. "If we stay out of its aura for too long, we begin to die."

J.C. frowned. "This subversion of life and death. It is my fault. None of this would have happened had I not made such terrible mistakes in my duty."

"It's your father's fault," the General growled, "He's the one who sent the meat-eor."

J.C. was confused. "I know that thou hast some difficulties with pronunciation, as thou dost not have lips, but didst thou say meteor or meat-eyeore?"

"It was a festering ball of meat from space. What else would we call it?"

J.C. thought about his father's true form and shuddered. It would make sense that YHWH would craft a colossus of biological detritus to hurl at the planet, since the creature had so very much bubbling, shifting flesh to spare. The meat-eor must be stopped at any cost, but in order to defy his father's will, he would need something powerful, and that was the black cross, the corrupted stave of creation. He was certain his father would be searching for it as well, and promised himself to be on his guard.

"How will we get back inside the volcano?" J.C. asked.

"How did you get out?" Myron countered.

J.C. shook his head. "That way is no good. When I escaped the cave, it collapsed and closed up again."

Myron thought a moment, and addressed Eoraptor, who was pacing back and forth. "Can we get through the peak? Up near where you once lived?"

Eoraptor sadly stared off into the middle distance. Finally, the smaller, much older dinosaur blinked a few times. "Everything up there was destroyed. Everything except me and the artifact I brought down from the mountain. They ruined all of it. We will simply have to go through the mammal village. That is the only way I know of to get in."

Jurassichrist

As they travelled up the mountain side, lights became apparent, and clear signs of the mammalian civilization blossomed around them. The hallmarks of a primitive rural society dotted the land, a silo for grain, gardens with strange irrigation infrastructures, and even crude dwellings. Convenience technology lit up these sites, with press-on lights and strings of twinkling, singing holiday bulbs creating a tapestry of gaudy illumination. They saw no mammals, as they travelled, most of the nighttime tasks accomplished by monotasking robots like gutter cleaners and floor sweepers. The mammals had been gifted technology far beyond their ability to understand, but it was clear that it was fundamentally changing their development. Their society was progressing faster than it should be. Most of them hadn't even learned to walk upright yet, and here they were with robotic discs that mopped their floors. YHWH was enslaving them, getting them hooked and addicted to convenience, and not allowing them to naturally discover these innovations for themselves through a billion years of trial and error. There was one source for the things that made their lives possible. "Nothing is impossible with God. His power makes all things possible." Had he really said that to his people? Never again, he swore to himself, as he continued moving through the shadows with his new friends. Mortals had to learn that they could be their own gods.

"All right, back to thought-based communication. We're getting close, now." Myron's clear voice rang through the minds of his companions. The four of them stopped behind a small grove of trees. The General was so large, he stuck out like a hill, and had to hold his breath to remain still enough to pretend to be just a part of the landscape.

Ahead, the structures increased in density, forming what appeared to be a village. Do-it-yourself neon sign kits and programmable L.E.D. signs spelled out various stores and entertainments in what appeared to be a sort of business district in the village square. All around this, dark homes stretched out for a parasa or more, silent and still in the middle of the night. There appeared to be a few mammals about, even this late, staggering drunkenly from one hovel to the next. One, a badger-like creature, came plodding out of a stone building marked as "SHAM-WOW BAR AND DANCEATERIA." It stood shakily on its hind legs, stopping just outside the front door, and puked into a nearby refuse pile. It laughed a seedy sort of giggle and pushed off the wall, stumbling in the other direction, as a tiny circular robot puttered by and tried to vacuum up the vomit, but mostly succeeded in smearing it around on the ground.

Two more mammals, both long-nosed quadrupeds, rolled out of a circular dome, arguing about something in their high-pitched, squealing dialect. The sign above the door read "MILOSH'S FUCK CLUB." A wolf with one eye stuck its head out the door and growled at the pair of smaller mammals, who chittered and hissed as they skittered away. It appeared to be either a matter of an unsettled bill or a threesome gone horribly awry.

"What else do these creatures do? They fight, fornicate, and feed."

General Arius held in a snort. His thoughts even sounded derisive. "Fucking mammals. I mean . . . not you, J.C. You're one of the good ones."

If nothing else, J.C. could take solace in the fact that his first visit to Earth had helped shape humans into more ethical and loving beings. Watching history from his home plane taught him those positive vibes hadn't lasted forever, but that was the whole point of coming back. A corrective measure. A reminder that people should be nice to each other, and not be assholes. If this was the state of proto-humanity now, how terrible would it be a few hundred millions years hence?

"General, you'll need to stay here," said Eoraptor, sadly. "Any closer and there will be no hiding you."

General Arius scowled, his huge snarling face downturned in annoyance. "There is a large part of me that wants to stage a full on assault and just crush as many of them as we can. Take the fight to them. Show them we're not extinct, nor will we go quietly."

"There are more than just this village, General. They would come in greater numbers, and we cannot risk the lives of those dinos back at the base." Myron's plumage stood on end. J.C. could tell that the ceratops was nervous. He looked like a feather duster with a face.

After securing the general in the deepest part of the tiny wooded area, the trio of J.C., Eoraptor, and Myron moved toward the center of the village, staying on the side streets to avoid excess light. It took them only a few minutes before they reached a sign that read "CAUTION." Ahead, there were a number of similar signs, crossed and wrapped with yellow tape. They were guarding an opening in the hillside, deep and black, that wound into the mountainside.

"That's it," Myron thought, "That's our way in."

Slowly, carefully, the trio snuck into the opening of the shaft. It was pitch black, and would have to remain that way for the moment, at least until they had gotten far enough in to avoid detection from passersby.

"Why all the caution signs?" asked J.C.

In answer, a low rumble shook the walls and clods of dirt rained down on the heads of the adventurers.

"This area has always been extremely active," Eoraptor said. "It no longer blows up. It falls down."

The immense weight of the mountain atop them made all three creatures shudder, as they worked their way further into the passage. The tunnel sloped down. A familiar smell hit J.C. as the tunnel thinned out. It reminded him of the first encounter he'd had with the mammals, the odor of shit and sex and rot. But, this was a stale and desiccated scent, the musty aroma of things long abandoned.

The dinosaurs told J.C. more of the story as they descended. The mammals had left the tunnels ages ago, but before they had done so, they had thrived and burst forth like a plague upon the surface. Their numbers came from the secret development they had been undergoing for those many eons, gaining the ability to use the technological bits and bobs supplied to them by on high. Traps and obstacles would be plentiful here, for it was unlikely anything had been disarmed when the mammals exited their previous home.

The tunnels were much larger than J.C. had remembered, and decked out with a variety of old, rusting machines and mechanisms. Everything from personal hygiene to gardening tools to cleaning products and cooking conveniences were stuck to the walls like the tunnels had been an American casual dining restaurant.

J.C. led the way toward the heart of the volcano. In his long suspension as a particle, he was unable to get his bearings or use his senses, so he felt a bit defeated by the irony of having lived in this place for millions of years and still not knowing his way around.

Jurassichrist

Suddenly, the style of their surroundings changed. Dirt tunnels gave way to carved stone chambers, some of which had decorative tapestries on the wall, and posters advertising various malt beverages, and sexy mammals using sponges to wash large stone wheels in the sun. Ahead, there were actual archways. This area was far less crude than anything they had seen previously. There appeared to be pipes for some kind of air or water to flow through. If they had figured out hydraulics or pneumatics already, what else was down here?

J.C. was unsettled. "This reminds me of the Romans. This level of civilization shouldn't have been able to happen for another hundred million years. The forced evolution worked. There could be any number of dangers down here."

"We should be extremely careful," said Myron.

As he said this, the three heard a distinct click. Eoraptor looked down and sighed. A broken tripwire lay underneath his clawed foot. "Oh, pterodactyl shit."

Slots dropped open on both sides of the tunnel and a cavalcade of nasty looking serrated spears fired from the walls, heading straight for the intruders hearts.

Michael Allen Rose

"Get out of the way!" cried J.C. as he dove sideways, the rapidly approaching metal spear tips only inches away from turning the trio into corpses.

𝔅𝔬𝔬𝔨 18

𝔄 **spear slammed** into J.C. hitting him just below the ribs. He flew back into the opposite wall, with the pointed end jammed deep inside him. J.C. screamed in pain and anger. This was the same spot he had been stabbed during his crucifixion, and getting speared is just one of those things that, even if it's happened to you before, you never really get used to it.

His heroic dive had saved Eoraptor from taking a spear through the skull, which would have ended his life despite his familiarity with the golden cross. The small dinosaur looked agog at the human god who had saved him, and bowed. "Thank you, mammal. I don't know what to say."

"Myron? Are you hurt?" J.C. rolled his shoulder over with a groan, taking care not to press on the weapon still protruding from his abdomen.

"Only a little," Myron said. The ceratops was standing up, pinned to the wall, with two spears thrust through the bony ridge behind his head. A few inches to the left or to the right, and he would have been skewered through a nostril and given a messy pike-based lobotomy. "I think I'm losing a lot of blood. I see stars."

J.C. carefully stood and braced himself against the wall. This was going to hurt. With a yelp, he jammed the end of the spear into the crease where the wall met the floor and pulled with both hands, yanking the spear out of his side and spraying a mess of holy blood and gore across a nearby tapestry depicting a group of opossums worshipping a television screen.

The two dinosaurs turned so white that it was obvious even beneath their feathered exteriors. "Are you going to be all right?" Eoraptor asked.

"I'll heal. Let's help Myron. He won't."

While J.C. used his holy magical strength to hold up the squat but hefty ceratops, Eoraptor gripped the poles with his teeth and wrenched them free. The spear tips had pierced the bone of the ceratopsian ridge, but there was little blood. Still, it looked uncomfortable, two ragged holes piercing Myron's main defensive structure.

J.C. fingered the tips. They were razor sharp, and serrated like combat knives. This was no ordinary metal—this was steel—the mammals had been given a way to refine steel from iron and carbon. Echoes of advertisements past floated through his head: "It's made from one-hundred-percent stainless steel!"

"Father," he muttered, already looking ahead for more traps.

They approached a tall doorway that had been sealed with a large, steel panel. J.C. meditated, trying to feel the vibrations of the black cross. Although he was surrounded by corruption, the signal the powerful artifact was emitting was like a spotlight among fireflies. "It's definitely up ahead," he said, running his fingertips over the cold steel door. "Dost thou think they sealed this part of the volcano off back when it was still in danger of erupting?"

"Makes sense," said Eoraptor, looking over the carvings.

"Can you read them, ancient one?" Myron asked.

"We're all pretty ancient now, to be fair," Eoraptor sarcastically replied, "but yes, I can make some of it out. Some of it is based on their old scratchings from when they'd barely begun to huddle together." The symbols showed a variety of glyphs, evidence of perhaps the first written language that mammals had ever invented. "It appears to be about this door . . . hmmm . . . beware all who enter here . . . this place is sacred to the Cenozoic Resistance . . . blah blah blah . . . "

"You can't read it?" asked J.C.

"No, it says blah, blah, blah." Eoraptor pointed to the mammalian symbol for "blah." "It continues: No warranty expressed or implied. Product owner is responsible for all liabilities and casualties resulting from use of Steel Door 3000. Warning . . . once Steel Door 3000 is installed, do not use Steel Door 3000 as door, unless you have completed disarming service C. See instruction manual A-4."

"Is this supposed to be a door?" Myron asked.

There was no visible knob or lever on this side of the steel door. No holes or dents marred the surface. It was implacable, silent, smooth, and perfect.

"Does it say anything else? Can thou read further instructions?"

Eoraptor peered closer. "Let me see. Something about danger . . . traps . . . possibly a curse? The sign above the door, however, reads: DUNGEON OF GYGAX."

"Does it tell us how it shall be opened?"

"That, it does not." Eoraptor said, with a nod.

"What's this?" J.C. had found a series of tiny holes next to the framework. It was like someone had taken a pin and made rows and columns.

Myron's eyes lit up. "It's a voice reactive operating system! We used them in the Wrap, although I doubt very much this one is tuned to the hum."

"There must be a password!" J.C. spoke louder, clearly directing his speech into the speaker. Soon, all three were trying words.

"Mammal! Disgusting! Password! One two three four five six! Your mother's maiden name! The name of your first pet! Butt stuff! Fourth edition sucked!"

Nothing worked. Myron leaned against the steel, deep in thought. As soon as he put his weight on it, the door creaked and fell in with a crash, raising a dust cloud from the long unused passageway.

"Oh."

Apparently nobody had bothered to hook up the Steel Door 3000 correctly. Sure enough, just inside the door was a note, stuck to the frame, printed on some kind of parchment paper. It appeared to show instructions on how to set the thing up. It was covered in drawings of dicks and other doodles, which assuredly weren't any less rude.

"Shall we?" J.C. led the way into the mountain's interior.

The group descended into a small carved tunnel, surrounded on every side by cooled granite. Clearly, the mammals had dug these tunnels in ancient times. A large boulder stood in the middle of the path. It was of a strange shape, with twenty sides, all bearing a number.

"Oh no," Myron muttered.

"What is it?"

The mammalologist turned. "I was afraid of this. This is an ancient rite of the mammals, used to protect sacred and special places. They call it an RPG: 'Ritualistic Protection of Genus,' although sometimes it is otherwise known as a 'Ridiculous Plotting Gimmick'. We'll have to play roles and find our way through their maze to receive our treasure."

Jurassichrist

"Yes, I am familiar with RPGs. Millions of years hence, during a period known as the Satanic Panic, the rite of the RPG shall lead many young humans down the path of heavy metals and paganism. So, mammals art nerds. Wonderous. What do we do? Create characters?" asked J.C. "I shalt double class as a human wizard cleric with a complex backstory and a natural distrust of hobgoblins."

"Well, that's an option. Or, if we roll that stone, depending on the number that comes up, it should show us the way through."

"I see," said J.C. as he limbered up his shoulders. "Well, luckily one of my critical skills is rolling boulders." The lord heaved and pushed the large stone icosahedron. It tumbled over and landed on a 14. A weird glow surrounded the number and the path before them lit up with battery-operated push lights coming to life every few yards. The floor down here was covered with Magic Step clean mats, held in place by Rug Gripper Stoppers. It was a clearance extravaganza, with the "extra" being "danger," and the "vaganza" being a rug that could kill you.

A bit further along, the path split, but J.C. could still feel the emanations from the black cross, and kept his group on target. Soon, they arrived at a locked door.

"Do you have any open spells?" Myron asked J.C.

"Not really. I can turn thine water into wine, walk on water, raise the dead, guidance, light, protection from evil . . . and I have a magic missile that is quite impressive, but locks are not my specialty."

"He's a cleric, but clearly dual classing," said Eoraptor.

"What?" asked Myron, just before the door flew open and they were confronted with a very large rat.

"Well, this is dire," said J.C. as the rat hissed and leaped at them.

Myron turned and swung his tail, which featured a mace-like club at the end of it, and smashed the rat. Everyone waited expectantly.

"What art thou all waiting for? What happened?"

Myron smiled at his human friend, quizzically. "We are in the midst of the ritual now. Rules must be followed." The dinosaur gestured at the stone die.

J.C. pushed the rock again, and it rolled over a few times before landing on a 20. As soon as it did, the rat exploded into a fountain of organs and plasma.

"Nice roll." Eoraptor nodded. "You're a surprisingly decent fighter, Myron."

The trip continued into the next room, where the rat had made its lair.

"The mammals we may encounter here are far more primitive than those on the surface," explained Myron. "They have probably been down here, growing in the darkness for generations."

The room terminated in another hallway, but it was blocked off by a magnetic hands-free screen door. J.C. raised his arms, and the two sides parted like a sea, allowing them to pass by unharmed. Everywhere they looked, As Seen On TV products had been installed. They dodged flying cleaning devices and leaped over self-guiding mops, stepping around carefully camouflaged pits covered with imitation grass.

Soon, they came upon another door, locked tight. A dog turd was nearby, provoking a look of disgust from Myron. "Eww! Ewwwww! Icky!" the dinosaur squealed. As disgusting as it was, though, something about it seemed artificial. It was too shiny, even in the dim fluorescent of the tunnels. Someone suggested they play rock-paper-scissors to decide who would pick it up, which lasted three rounds before Eoraptor, having had enough, just kicked the turd aside. Sure enough, the door's key had been hidden underneath, protected by the idea that surely no intruder would touch a piece of poop.

Finally, they reached a lower chamber that appeared to be a dead end. Inside were a number of ugly mammals, gnawing on a pile of eggs. "Those . . . are dinosaur eggs," said Myron, with great horror.

Indeed, the greasy mammals were sucking out the albumen, allowing placental fluid to drip down their hairy chins.

"We know that some dinosaurs still survive . . . the crocodilians, for example . . . and our brother birds . . . these creatures must have raided a nest. Sheer brutality." A single golden tear ran down Eoraptor's feathered face. The mammals, moving with a quickness that belied their grotesque bulging bellies, jumped to their clawed feet.

"Fresh meats!" one chittered.

"Thunder lizards? They gone. How they here now?"

"Who cares," growled the largest. "We eat first, ask questions later."

"Quickly, J.C., roll the stone! They are still bound by their rules here!"

J.C. struck the edge of the icosahedron, sending it skipping across the uneven floor. It came up with a 1 on top.

"We have initiative!" screeched the smallest of the gaggle, as they leaped forward to engage the trio in battle.

Two of the creatures latched onto Myron. The ceratops roared and swung around wildly, using his bulk to try smashing them. He fell to the floor, struggling to turn the tables. Meanwhile, two more attacked Eoraptor, and were engaged in a agile dance of death with his teeth and claws as they nipped at his legs.

The largest one leaped toward J.C., fangs bared.

With one thunderous punch, J.C. laid the mammal out, flat on his back, unconscious. "I am not bound by your rules." As the mammals looked on in astonishment, J.C. ran around in a circle, clobbering each of the beasts in turn. "That's not fair, you lost the roll. That was a critical fail!" cried the smallest as J.C. drop kicked it into the wall. It slid down soundlessly, and twitched in the corner.

"That was amazing, J.C.," stammered Myron.

"I find that rituals only have the power that we impart upon them," J.C. said. "Come now, let us go forward before they awaken."

The dungeon became less well maintained as they travelled downward, until finally, the carefully carved tunnels abruptly stopped and gave way to a web of limestone cracks and fissures, far too small for the dinosaurs.

"I have to go on alone," said J.C., dropping to his hands and knees.

The two dinos were gravely concerned. "What if we can't find you again? What if you're hurt?"

"Wait here for a while. Perhaps an hour or so. Once that time has passed, thou should return to the surface. Wait for me there a while longer. If I am injured, I can heal. It just takes time."

Voicing their dissent, the two dinos sullenly helped J.C. crawl into an upper tunnel, the one where the strongest signal was present. Somewhere up ahead was the chamber in which he had spent so much time, wasted. He would find the corrupted stave and spite his father's plan, even if it killed him, yet again.

The atmosphere of these lower chambers was familiar somehow. The dripping water, the

scent of cave moss and mineral leavings, even
the chill of the subterranean air, all gave J.C. a
shiver. Passing over a series of rocky
outcroppings, J.C. entered a large cavern, and
summoned light from his holy palm holes,
using them like flashlights. He was on a ledge
overlooking a crystal-clear subterranean lake.
Below, a variety of bright white, blind cave fish,
swam about in the water. Strange, alien
crustaceans skittered around in and out of the
water, carrying tiny bits of moss and lichen.
Minerals had built up in places, leaving trails of
orange, pink, and white down the walls like a
celestial painting had been made here.

This was how creation was supposed to be.
Pure. Natural. J.C. sighed, remembering how it
had been at the beginning, when light and
darkness were separated, and they had
conjured up all manner of cool organisms to
populate their little experimental terrarium. No
egos were at play, no treachery. Even YHWH,
at the time, had been jovial and excited,
thinking about the possibilities. As they set the
evolution project into motion, they enjoyed
long conversations about what might result.
Hidden agendas seemed impossible at the time.
Everyone just wanted to watch mortals

flourish, to see what they became, to allow them to learn to become their own gods, free from the pettiness and strife that marked those who lived with the inevitability of death.

But, something had gone wrong along the way. War, slavery, exploitation, power, it was difficult to watch. That was why J.C. had proposed sending some celestials along once in a while to help them out. Guides, teachers, little corrective actions from management, just until they figured it out for themselves. He had been perhaps the most famous one, but there had been many others who had impacts both great and very small: Abraham, Muhammad, The Dalai Lama Lhamo Thondup, Thag: maker of fire, and Thomas P. MacGregor of Cincinnati, Ohio.

J.C. worked his way down the wall. His muscles ached, especially his core, which was still smarting from the slowly healing spear wounds. He dropped the last few feet to the ground, crouching at the edge of the water. The thrumming emanations of the black stave were loud enough that they shook his eardrums.

Down below where the fish swam, stuck into a crevasse, the black cross crackled with corrupt energy. The shape of it appeared as an inky midnight black, even against the shadows of the lightless depths.

J.C. took a huge breath and plunged into the icy cold water, paddling toward the bottom as quickly as he could. The light coming from his hands caused tiny animals to scatter, the light serving as a menacing alien invader in this place. This water was untouched by any civilization, natural and perfect. The black cross stuck out like the abomination it was.

J.C. wrapped his arms around the cross beams, and felt a surge of energy ripple through him. This was truly twisted magic, a degradation of holy power that could surely unmake things just as easily as its golden brethren could create them. He braced himself against the lake's stone floor and pulled with all his might. Slowly, the cross unstuck, then finally, with a massive burst of trapped bubbles, it came free, and J.C. quickly kicked his way to the surface.

He dragged the cross to the edge of the lake, and still breathing heavily, he rolled up onto the shore, pulling the cross with him. It blazed with a deep purple light that made his robes glow. It may be too late to save this space and time from doom, but timelines were made to be altered and now that he had this power, he might be able to go back and fix it.

As he lay, catching his breath, he heard an evil hiss.

"See? The TV prophesied that we would find him here. Don't let him leave this place."

A dozen or more tiny yellow eyes shone in the darkness above him. He heard the sounds of several tiny guns being readied to fire, and closed his eyes.

Book 19

"**March, hairless ape.**" J.C. stumbled upward through the tunnel, trying not to trip over the rocks in the dim light. The mammals training their weapons on him had no such difficulty, being equipped with the ability to see in the dark. They called him a hairless ape. That meant that somewhere, apes existed, which meant that evolution had sped up by at least sixty million years or so. It was also disturbing how well they had picked up human languages. To his ears, the dialect sounded like twenty-first century American English. It was lucky he was omniscient in his grasp of human languages, otherwise he'd have to have hoped for Aramaic, which was fairly unlikely.

There were eight of them, all armed to the teeth, and even armed *on* their teeth, having covered them with As Seen On TV Perfect Smile Veneers that had been shaped into fangs. The weapons they held were modified salad shooters and hose attachments. One of them had an immersion blender, a nasty bit of work, that had been duct taped to the handle of a Swiffer. He poked J.C. in the back to keep him moving, whispering threats about turning it on and making a tall glass of animal juice.

J.C. had to crawl through the shorter tunnels, slowing their progress and making the mammals hiss and boo. It felt very much like the time he had to climb the hill before his crucifixion, only at least this time he wasn't carrying a couple hundred pounds of dead wood. Of course, he also didn't have a Simon of Cyrene around to help him carry his burden. Luckily, the black cross was surprisingly light, likely due to its celestial construction and magical material properties. The mammals, still more comfortable on their four legs than standing bipedally, had no trouble, and let him know it.

"You think you get away, but nope! We too smart for you."

Jurassichrist

"How didst thou know to find me?" J.C. said, hefting himself and the black artifact up over a large rock.

"It easy!" screeched one of the creatures. "Tee vee tells us you come for magic stick, so we wait for you. You get it from fish pool, we get you!"

"What art thou planning to do with me?"

The mammals snickered and chortled in response. "Move," snarled the one with the Swiffer stick of blending, poking J.C. again.

J.C.'s hopes were further dashed upon crawling out of the tunnel into the chamber where he had left Myron and Eoraptor. He tried to calculate the time in his head, hoping that they had waited for a bit and left, as he had suggested. As if reading his mind, the one with the modified Swiffer jabbed at him once more, saying, "You wonder where lizards go? You think they get away? No, we find them first. We sneaky. Play numbers game. They big and strong, but we are many. Practically drown them in our corpses! We follow you, and catch them by surprise."

Grimacing and sweating, J.C. closed his eyes, trying to retain his peaceful tone so as not to further agitate these psychopaths. "Where are they? Thou didst not hurt them?"

"You see soon enough, magic ape. Faster now. Pick up pace."

The dungeon loomed ahead. "Stop," they commanded, and halted in the chamber, before one of the mammals walked in front of the group, holding its paws skyward. The thing spit some bizarre chant, comprised of obscure and esoteric syllables.

"What's happening?" J.C. asked his captors.

Between shushing him, one answered: "Quiet. He dungeon master. He metagaming."

The creature finished speaking and waited. There was a heavy silence, as though the air changed. A previously unseen tunnel suddenly opened up in one of the walls. The group continued their trek, only the passage led straight through the dangers, in a very linear path. There were even benches with blankets along the way for travelers to take extended rest periods.

"To thee I say, bullshit," J.C. muttered, dragging the black cross along behind him. It crackled and buzzed, sending tiny shivers up his spine. It took little time to arrive in the upper caverns, and by the time they reached the entrance, a massive bonfire was roaring in the center of town. Someone fed the fire and the flames roared up, sending embers spiraling up into the sky.

The heat was intense. Mammals of all shapes and sizes were situated around the fire, dancing, drinking, and carousing. When they saw the hunting party approaching, a loud cheer went up.

The two dinosaurs were nearby, but looked worse for wear. Myron was tied up in dozens of Slackers Ninjaline climbing ropes, secured with SuperRope Cinches (As Seen On TV, naturally). His face was bloody, and there were more dents and cracks in his bone plate. His feathers were matted with sweat, blood, and saliva. Eoraptor had been fitted with a Petrainer Remote Dog Training Collar, and small mammals were taking turns shocking the shit out of him whenever he dared to move outside the bounds of the circle they'd drawn on the ground. Everywhere, mammals leaned out of windows, throwing garbage and shouting jeers, as J.C. was marched toward the fire. As soon as his friends saw him, they hung their heads in despair.

"They were upon us as soon as you left," said Myron, shaking. "We hoped that you might somehow escape, but it appears our hopes remain unfounded."

Michael Allen Rose

J.C. frantically processed strategies for escape. There had to be a way, hadn't there? His third coming couldn't end this ignobly. As he was rudely shoved next to the two dinosaurs, he tried to exude a cheerful hope, but it was flagging as the mammals cheered again, parting and making space.

A sweaty aardvark thing in a yellow polyester leisure suit moved a box into the cleared area and stood on top of it next to the fire. He addressed the crowd.

"Long time has finally come to pass! We listen as tee vee tells us some day these ones come and wreck up the place. Fuck up all! But no, we never allow, we catch criminals before they can ruin everything! Now there no stopping us from being most powerful, happy, sexy! After this, tee vee promise what we already know. We center of universe. We most important creation! Earth given to us to do with what we please. Can burn old bones to make vehicles that go fast! Can make products for to make us even more sexy beautiful! Can get rid of fat without changing diet! Everything we want, we get!"

The crowd roared its approval.

"Distraction."

"What?" J.C. asked, turning to his allies. Both Myron and Eoraptor shook their heads, confused. J.C. looked around, but there was nobody else speaking either.

"You . . . distraction."

The voice was coming from inside his mind.

"You need to create a distraction."

It was the gruff voice of the Spinosaurus, General Atrius. He had not been discovered, and now he must be observing the scene from somewhere nearby. Perhaps there was hope after all.

"A distraction?" J.C. thought, as hard as he could. "What kind of distraction?"

General Atrius's thoughts came through fuzzy and filled with static. It reminded J.C. of his first time inside the mammal tunnels, when the thought communication network went down. It was at that moment he realized: YHWH was jamming the signals. That's why this mountain was the central hub of the magical television. It was his central nexus of power on Earth. Of course he would have holy signal jammers active. Anything he could do to disrupt the dinosaurs' cohesiveness would serve his ends. That omniscient bastard. It was so much worse underground, and that made sense. The signals that YHWH was using to generate the tee vee content must be quite powerful to reach all the way from the celestial plane to deep beneath the Earth soil, and he wouldn't want anyone interrupting or hijacking them. The lord was a l33t haxxor indeed.

Radio silence filled the void inside J.C.'s mind. There was no time to wait for further clarification. The aardvark was finishing his speech.

" . . . will finally prevail when terrorists have been burned to ashes! Hail Cenozoic Resistance!" The crowd cheered, holding their paws, hooves, and feet up in salute. J.C. felt strong clawed hands from behind gripping his sides, and he was torn away from the black cross with great force. He tried to hold onto it, not wanting to lose it again, especially if he was about to be obliterated by fire (yet again) but it was too late. His wrists and feet were bound. They even tied the ropes through the holes in his extremities, making the knots very secure.

"Whip him! Scourge him! Make him blood rain!" J.C. felt something lightly smack into his rump, and then against his lower calves. There was a moment of silence. "What that?"

Another small voice: "No have whip. Use

grab-it ultra." Sure enough, a chipmunk with acne was standing nearby, having trouble balancing a long grabbing tool on a plastic stick. When the critter noticed J.C. looking at him, he grimaced, pulled the handle again, and pinched the Lord's thigh.

"Cut it out," J.C. snapped. At least the Romans had known what they were doing.

Myron and Eoraptor were placed on either side of J.C., situated next to the licking flames. The heat was intense, and immediately Myron struggled against his bonds. It was no use, as he and J.C. were tied up tight with cheap As Seen On TV appurtenances. Eoraptor looked terrified, having been blasted with electric shocks every time he moved or tried to speak.

"Any final words, hairless ape?" asked the aardvark thing, as his giggling minions readied themselves to push the trio into the bonfire.

It was time to act. J.C. turned to his companions. "Fear not. Verily I say unto thee, today shalt thou be with me in paradise." Echoing his experiences from his first coming, he closed his eyes and tapped into the power of the cosmos. Deep, in the very pit of his stomach, he felt power rising. This was an energy that he had only been able to find at the very bottom of the well of despair, when death seemed inevitable, and now he would unleash it once more.

Mirroring the events that would happen in a few million years (around 34 A.D., give or take) as he hung dying on a big wooden "t," darkness came over all the land. The sun was darkened, and the veil of the temple was torn down the middle. In this case, the veil was the sign for the MILOSH'S FUCK CLUB, which exploded into pink neon flames and fell into pieces, shattering and impaling several ugly mammals.

Screams and chaos abounded. The winds blew and the flames rose as the moon disappeared, then the stars blinked out, one by one. By firelight, a short distance away, what appeared to be a hill on the horizon suddenly moved.

General Arius came smashing through the village square with a blood-curdling roar, sending mammals and buildings flying. He gobbled up a whole group of mammals with one snap of his jaws, chewing noisily and allowing the gore to run down his chin for maximum fear effect. It worked—the mammals ran screaming, as the few that were armed tried to maintain a defensive line. It was useless against the rampaging Spinosaurus, who dwarfed even the largest buildings, and stomped and smashed through them with reckless abandon.

"Now, Eoraptor, thou must hurry while they pay us no attention!" J.C. whispered.

Eoraptor, as if waking from a trance of terror, quickly began to bite through the bonds holding his friends. Once he had finished, the trio moved away from the fire, with J.C. kicking and punching, Eoraptor taking snapping bites, and Myron slamming his tail into the frenzied mammals before them.

"That's for shocking me, you hairy little douche canoe!" growled the elderly raptor as he bit down, snapping a striped mammal between his jaws and knocking its remote control out of its severed hand. He stomped on it over and over again. "That'll show them!"

"Come, we must hurry," said Myron, gasping with exhaustion.

"GO!" roared General Arius, just before he ate a house.

"Help me with this!" J.C. yelled over the screams, the sounds of salad shooters buzzing to life, and the loud open-mouth chewing of the Spinosaurus. "We cannot leave without the stave!"

Myron grabbed the long end of the black cross, and with Eoraptor leading the way, they ran for cover.

"They're getting away—" they heard a mammal squeak, just before a very loud stomp cut the sound off.

"GET TO SAFETY AND UNMAKE ALL OF THIS!" The General was roaring in rage and pain.

The General was flailing around, doing massive damage to the mammal village, but they had regrouped and were now trying to surround the massive dinosaur with their strange weapons. They had some kind of electric tasers on poles that they were using to corral General Arius. The village square was a pool of gore, with clumps of hair and bones flying left and right as the Spinosaurus-powered slaughter carried on, but more mammals were coming now, woken by the shouting or finally having armed themselves.

"We must save him," said J.C., thinking of what powers he might be able to pull up in his exhausted and hurt state. The sky was lightening even now, the clouds parting and the moon shining once more. He attempted to summon an arsenal similar to the one he had originally landed in the Cretaceous with, but his power was sucked dry and not even a pistol would form. He tried to grit his teeth and make fire to throw at the mammals, but his hands simply smoked. His wounds began bleeding again, tiny micro-tears opening in the muscle as he strained. His healing was slow. Everything was slow. He needed a long rest, otherwise his mortal form would start falling apart at the seams if he tried to do something with his holy magic even as simple as multiplying some bread.

Eoraptor bumped J.C. with his head. "I'm sorry, J.C., but we must leave. Now. There is no time."

"But they shalt kill him!"

"He knows what he is doing. He is fulfilling his mission. The only way to save him now is to ensure that the timeline changes so that none of this ever happens." Myron pulled J.C.'s robes and ushered him toward the safehouse.

Their head start didn't last for long—the sounds of battle behind them faded, but very quickly they could hear a hunting party had formed and were yelling for them to stop. The trio ran, sweating and scrabbling, only a stadium ahead of their pursuers, until finally they came upon the appropriate spot. Myron sent out a thought bomb: "OPEN UP, IT'S US!" Just then, a series of saws, knives, and cleavers, comprising the Outdoor Edge Game Processor kit, flew through the air and raked Myron's hide with severe lacerations. The ceratops fell forward, and lay still.

"Myron!" J.C. cried.

"Hurry, hurry . . . " Eoraptor was jumping back and forth, as the secret hatch slowly opened up in the ground before them.

J.C. knelt beside Myron, laying his hands on the dinosaur. "Be still." His hands glowed with a bright yellow light, but after only a few seconds, they blinked out and he grimaced in pain.

Myron turned his head, struggling for breath. "You don't have the power to save me. You must get inside."

"I'm getting all of you killed!" Jesus wept. "I can save you! I just need time."

"We don't have time!" Eoraptor cried, as the door finally opened enough for him to squeeze through. The aged but agile dino pulled the black cross into the hatch with him. There were sounds of scrambling and many voices inside. "Close it! Now! Come on, J.C.! Get inside!"

Jurassichrist

J.C. looked down at Myron, then up at the pack of mammals now closing in. He shuddered to think what might have happened to the General. These mammals had broken away from the village and tracked them here, and were preparing for another round of razor sharp death. They were howling and cheering, with bandoliers of sharp kitchen knives and hunting kits.

Myron squeezed J.C.'s holy hand. "You can't save everyone."

"Yes, I can! I am the way! This be my truth! I am thy light! That is my thing!"

"You can either try to save me now, or save everyone later. Not both. You know that."

Allowing bloody tears to fall freely, and making a sign of blessing over the dying dinosaur, J.C. hopped up and sprinted the last few yards, diving into the slowly closing hatch. He rolled to the floor in a heap.

"Here they come!" cried a dinosaur, as sounds of gunfire burst from above. The dinosaurs were trying to repel the invaders as the hatch closed. "They're getting in! Oh reptilicus!"

He was in the eye of a maelstrom, with scaly feet and hairy hooves stomping around him, and the clashing sounds of battle. The hatch ground closed with a gritty crunch, and several yelps of pain were heard, even through the thick metal door, as the second wave of pursuers were flattened in the mechanism. He looked up just as a young Tyrannosaurus Rex bit one of the intruders into two pieces. Another mammal, a large wolf-like monstrosity, ripped the throat out of a raptor and tackled another bipedal dino to the ground before discharging a taser attachment and sending it into spasms. It turned and growled in J.C.'s face, and opened its mouth to take a bite of the savior's eye sockets.

Its eyes suddenly went glassy, and its jaw went limp. The mammal fell to the ground, bleeding out of its mouth, its brain destroyed. Standing behind the creature, J.C. was pleased to see his old acquaintance, the Compsognathus Officer Spingle. The vicious little dinosaur was wearing some kind of jaw extension. It grinned a steely, shiny smile. J.C. had been on the receiving end of those teeth himself, and as he picked himself up, he nodded in thanks. The bite pressure of the officer had exploded the mammal's skull.

"It's nice to be on the same side, for once," J.C. muttered.

Jurassichrist

The few other mammals that had penetrated the dinos defenses had been dealt with, but there was a heavy toll. Several members of the receiving team were injured or dead, and Eoraptor explained with some solemnity that even the golden cross that had kept the dinosaurs alive for so long was unable to bring back mortals from beyond the veil of death.

J.C. promised to do what he could for the sick and dying, but before he could protest, Eoraptor had ordered a couple of friendly Hadrosaurs to cart J.C. off and put him in bed. He was about to say that he could keep going, that there was no time, that he had to get back and try another coming to make it all okay, but before he could speak word number one, he had passed out, the black cross cradled in his arms.

Observers would later say that the energy crackling between the holy man and the corrupt artifact felt like a battle for the fate of the universe. It may have been exactly that, and whomever had the stronger will might change the reality of everything that had been, was, and would be.

Book 20

Over the next few days, the remaining dinosaurs worked hard helping J.C. and supplying him with various materials. Everything left in the bunker that was made of wood was piled up in the main room, where J.C. selected the best pieces and shaped them with his skills. The dinosaurs wove the leaves of plants, many of which they had maintained in a makeshift terrarium, into cloth. They used their hum to help shape and refine the ichor and oricalchum, sacrificing power to the least used parts of the bunker to energize the materials for J.C. His weakened magic could only conjure up the simplest of tools, but hammers, lathes and saws were enough. His experience as a carpenter was coming in handy.

The project itself was fairly complex. First, they built a sturdy crucifix that was also lightweight and flexible. They attached that to a suit of woven plant matter with details and notions constructed of their legendary metals. Mechanical stirrups were installed with simple latches so that carefully hammered oricalchum "nails" would move along a chosen path when triggered and press into wooden slots in the cross beam. This was all controlled by a handy thumb-switch, with a backup foot pedal that could be utilized by clicking one's heels together three times.

After three days, they stood back and looked upon their works.

"Try it on," Eoraptor prompted, gently.

J.C. strapped himself into the device. It was important that he be able to operate it without assistance, otherwise their plan would never work. He flexed his fingers and toes and placed his arms and legs into the harnesses they had built. The bottom of the cross was chopped so that it cut off just above the ground, allowing J.C. to walk normally, but acting as a stable base if he leaned back. He turned in a circle, and did some kung-fu moves to test his agility. Everything was in working order.

"Success. My friends, thou hast done wonders this day." J.C. rolled his shoulders forward, pulling the cross up like a backpack. "Go ahead, attach the stave."

A couple of dinosaurs with forelimbs capable of grasping picked up the black cross and fit it into the carved ridge they had made in the apparatus. It fit like a glove. The whole thing began to crackle with energy. A tingle sparked in the tips of J.C.'s toes, and carried up his legs, vibrating his spine and filling him with heat and pressure. It felt like his nerves were being shocked, like he'd smashed his funny bone into a wall, but all throughout his body. The power surged through him, electric crackles flying between his fingertips.

A gasp of awe exploded from the surrounding dinosaurs. At least, J.C thought it was a gasp of awe. It was bird-like and high-pitched, like a pelican had become stuck inside a tea kettle, but judging from the tired but happy faces on the dinosaurs, it seemed awe-like. (Historically speaking, it's a fact that dinosaurs loved to feel awe. In fact, it was their third favorite thing to feel, ranked just behind smug self-satisfaction at number two and the sense of warmth, peace, and tranquility when you are warm and dry inside the house during an intense rainstorm, also known as Chrysalism, in first place).

"I call it: The Crucifixer!"

They had essentially created a personal time machine for Jesus.

"If this works, once you go, you probably won't be able to find your way to this point in time and space. You'll have to seek out the moment of the extinction event and stop the meat-eor from striking," Eoraptor explained, as he patted J.C.'s shoulder.

"YHWH will surely know I am coming," said J.C. "His wrath is limitless and surely he will strike at thee with all the force of creation if this mission fails."

"Then, you cannot fail."

J.C. prepared himself mentally for yet another death, albeit by his own hand. This was going to be his third mortal death, unless of course he counted his time as a floating molecule and rebirth into his human form, which was kind of a death and rebirth cycle as well, even though he hadn't travelled back home to other layers of the multiverse. That meant the score was three deaths, with four births and or rebirths, three of which were resurrections. He readied himself for number four and waved good-bye to the refugees in the bunker.

As the dinosaurs solemnly stood by, J.C. fired up the Crucifixer on his back, stuck out his arms and grabbed the loops through which his wrists fit. He leaned back, letting his weight rest on the bottom beam, and popped his feet up as he toggled the thumb switch. The nails clicked through his palms, and he giggled as they tickled the holes there. They had measured down to the micron, and for once, it was nice not to feel the metal pounded through his own flesh.

There was a burst of black lightning, the smell of rain, a loud whoosh, and then J.C. disappeared.

J.C. opened his eyes to a field of clouds, but the sky wasn't the usual blue he was used to. Crimson streaks colored the air on a deep purple backdrop, as storms raged in the distance. This was a Zeus-style tantrum in progress, something that YHWH hadn't really done since the Old Testament days, but then had J.C. ever really known the *real* YHWH? The air burned in places, balls of fire hanging mid-air, seemingly fed by pure anger. A few ghosts, angels, and demons wandered here and there, taking in the devastation. The mere presence of otherworldly beings suggested that perhaps God was not present, which was strange, but a blessing for J.C.

"J.C.? Is that you?"

A powerful female voice beckoned from behind. J.C. turned, ready to leap into combat if necessary, but when he saw who the voice belonged to, he was quite glad he didn't act rashly.

Before him stood Ishtar, the gigantic Sumerian goddess of sex, war, and fertility. She was laughing, throwing bolts of energy around and sitting atop the decapitated, naked corpse of what appeared to be a recent lover. This was not surprising. Ishtar's lovers tended to last far longer *in* bed than they did post-coitus.

"Inanna?"

"Call me Ishtar, sweetie."

"What are you doing here?"

"Oh, the usual. Getting kind of bored, actually. I've already turned the rivers to blood, covered the Earth with storms, and tormented the people with disease. I'm thinking I might try turning some people into mongeese. Is it mongeese? Mongooses?"

"I mean, how is it that you've been given dominion here? This is not thy neighborhood."

This was true. Under normal circumstances, the deities stayed in their own portions of the celestial planes, maintaining their own experimental fishbowls of mortals, their own realms, and their own laws of the universe. They got together to play games and eat pot luck sometimes, but running rampant in another god's space was usually a definitive no-no.

"Your dad left. He said he didn't give a fuck what happened to the place," Ishtar said, plucking a juicy looking human out of a small bowl nearby and popping him into her mouth. "So, we're having a party!"

"Noooo!" the little man screamed, as he dangled from her fingertips, before she dropped him into her gullet, biting down with a snap.

"Baron Samedi is over there drinking rum, smoking cigars, and telling dirty jokes. You should say hi! Loki is here, Sheela Na Gigs is running around showing everyone her cunt. Hell, Pan is so drunk he shit on the coffee table! Woah, dude! Get a load of Chinnamasta!"

Chinnamasta, Hindu goddess of self-sacrifice, strolled by, leaving a red trail of slick gore behind her. She had cut off her own head and was enjoying parading around with it while three spurts of blood flowed from her open neck. As some sort of weird party trick, her severed head and two of her attendants, who were following close behind, were drinking the spurting blood, catching it in their mouths like thrown grapes. The other rampaging spirits howled with laughter, raising their glasses in a toast to debauchery.

Bidding the goddess adieu, J.C. travelled to the throne room, ready to fire up the Crucifixer if things went completely sideways. In God's throne room, alarm bells and sirens were going off. The voice of God was still sitting in the middle of the room at their desk, but various faces were panicked, screaming or on fire. Their many arms were hard at work, putting out conflagrations, polishing the furniture, sending onlookers skedaddling, and generally keeping the place intact.

"Vox, thou must know where my father has gone?"

The voice was already looking at J.C. but turned the eyes of several faces his way anyway, to prove they were paying attention. "Hello again, J.C. Nice to see you. Sorry that things are such a mess today. Your father has taken a vacation, and will not be back in the office until after the apocalypse. Would you like to leave a message?"

"Where is he?" growled J.C. while striking a kung-fu pose.

"I believe he's gone to the moment of the first apocalypse to ensure it goes correctly."

The first apocalypse? It had to be the meateor impact. YHWH was there to make sure nobody foiled his plan. Well, Jesus Christ of Nazareth (the town, not the band) would not stand idly by and watch God fuck up his planet. Manifesting adventurer's goggles on his forehead, J.C. pulled them down over his eyes with great gravitas.

"To adventure! Though I teleport through the valley of the shadow of death, I fear no God, for I am ready to kick thine ass! My rod and my staff, they comfort me," said J.C. as he kissed each of his closed fists for good luck.

His hands went through the loops and he pressed the button.

"I'll tell him you stopped by!" said the voice of God, waving their many hands.

He focused all his thoughts. It was going to

be quite a trick to arrive at the moment of the extinction. "First time lucky," he muttered, closing his eyes and feeling the nails enter his palm holes. There was no good way to navigate his jumps without a technical crew behind him helping ensure things went well. He would just have to concentrate on specific images and concepts, and try to steer himself to the right place and time. A tremendous flash of light and a crippling sense of speed later, J.C. opened his eyes.

𝕭𝖔𝖔𝖐 21

𝕹othing.

There was just, nothing.

A blank, white canvas, endless, boundless. It actually reminded J.C. of the universe before creation, and he wistfully reminisced with great fondness over the sense of infinite possibilities they had felt back then. Was it possible that he had gone back that far? No, that time and place was, well, *timeless*, so he couldn't have gone back there.

"Wahhhh! Wahhhh!" The cry came from behind him. J.C. spun around. He was facing a little house made of stone and thatched straw. More cries joined the first, and seconds later, a chorus of cries, all coming from inside the house.

Jurassichrist

Before J.C. could act, the front door opened, and a somewhat bent-over man of average height, with a grave and gentle gait, clambered out of the house and closed the door behind him. His face was long, and he squeezed his big eyes shut against the noise coming from the other side of the door. He had a brown complexion, his hair and beard were thick, black, and curly, and his countenance was melancholy and thoughtful. When he saw J.C., he stormed angrily toward the lord.

"You!"

"Me?"

The man strode up and poked Jesus in the chest with one long finger. "You leave-a me here with all-a these babies to take care? You son of a . . . can I blaspheme here?"

J.C. immediately knew where he was. "Hello, Dante." He had landed in purgatory, a gateway dimension between the planes. The population here was basically Dante Alighieri, an Italian poet from the late middle ages, and a whole heap of unbaptized babies.

"It wasn't my decision, Dante. It was God's call. How are you? How are the kids?"

"How-a you think they are? They cry all-a the time. I can't lactate, but they keep-a wanting a boob in-a the mouth. What am I supposed to do? We don't have to eat nothing here to survive, but try-a telling them-a that! They're babies! They don't listen to-a reason!"

Dante had written a pretty infamous tell-all book about the planes that J.C. and his pals trafficked in, and not everyone had been thrilled with the tabloid quality of the fact checking that had gone into his exposé. This had happily coincided with a major line item on the agenda about figuring out what to do with all the babies piling up in limbo. Dante had met one of the staff here, called Cato, who had showed him around "backstage" and when Cato was unceremoniously retired from existence for not shutting his yap, Dante had been put here to be a caretaker. The thing was, this place didn't really need a caretaker. There was nothing to mow, rake, polish, shovel, open, close, vent, clean, shine, or trim. There were just the damned babies. When Dante was told about his new job, he wasn't exactly pleased, but he was given a choice: either take the position, or end up like Cato, who had been systematically disassembled into his component parts and then trapped, in a form that was basically hot gas, in a small globe filled with anti-matter, so that he was constantly made and unmade from existence in perpetuity forever and ever, amen. Dante had suddenly found his fate more reasonable.

"I shall see what I can do about thou and thy child care needs, but first, hast thou seen my father?"

"You ask if I have-a gazed upon the very face of-a God?" Dante trembled, even as the babies cried louder. "I should say most certainly not, for no mortal has ever—"

"Yes, Dante, I know, thou art a supplicant in the eyes of the lord, blah blah blah. Lookest thou, I remember when you visited. Remember? You entered the Empyrean, the domain of God, and we blessed thee with holy light and made thou see roses? God took the form of three equally large circles occupying the same space? I was there? Dad was there? The holy spirit was floating around? It was a whole thing."

Dante blushed. "Oh, yes, that."

"What I mean is, hast thou seen the Lord thy God *since* then? Keepest thee in mind he may have appeared as a gibbering horror with tentacles and a multiplicity of eyeballs."

The crying was becoming inconceivably

distracting now. Dante shrugged and pointed over his shoulder. "Can you do something about this?"

J.C. sighed and waved his hands. Within seconds, the crying stopped. "It's the least I can do."

"What did you . . . ?" Dante tip-toed back to his front door and peered inside. The babies, the thousands and thousands of babies, all had a bottle in their tiny mouths, and every single bottle was filled with milk. "Oh, that is-a totally badass, Jesus."

"Thou art welcome," J.C. panted. It was probably worth it. Dante didn't really deserve this punishment, otherwise he'd have been sent to Hades or Hell or Hel or . . . come to think of it, most of the worst places in the multiverse began with the letter "h." Huh. "It is a combination of my turning water into things and my powers of multiplication. The drink should technically last forever, give or take."

"It's not-a . . . wine, is it?"

"No, worry thee not. Milk. I just had to split the metaphysical aspects of the concept of liquid into . . . never thou mind. Just be blessed. Now, about that God?"

"Come-a to think of it, the babies have been

crying an awful lot today. I thought-a I saw something outside-a the window earlier, but I thought-a that must be a trick of my imagination. But it-a looked like a mess, and it just travelled through and was on-a its way—there one second, gone the next."

"Did the creature do anything?"

"Like I said, it didn't really do-a anything, but kind of blink into existence and-a out again."

"Thank you, Dante," said J.C., before strapping himself back into his Crucifixer and firing up the machine. His mind had been a bit blank, before. This time he would try to picture where he had first landed, the prehistoric, muddy climes of the Mesozoic era.

"Wait just a minute," Dante called out. The sound of babies sucking their bottles increased, now harmonizing with sounds of puking, nonsensical singing, and the breaking out of random baby fights. "You've made a terrible mistake, lord! This isn't milk at all. You made an infinite supply of white chocolate martinis. I'm a-gonna have to deal with a billion drunk babies?"

J.C. blushed. "I'm so sorry! It's been a tough day! We all fall short of God's glorious standard!"

With a flash and a cacophonous burst of noise, J.C. was off through space and time again. Immediately, the babies began to cry, every single one of them (somewhere around six billion babies, at his last count) due to the noise, and their newly inebriated status. Dante leaned against the door and joined the crying multitude, just a little.

Jesus once again landed in mud, ruining yet another set of robes. This was promising though, reminiscent of his last descent to Earth.

"Finally," he said, pulling up his goggles. There were no dinosaurs here. In fact, he was surrounded by humans, many of which looked a lot like him. The smell was atrocious, dirt, smoke, and body odor permeating the entire layer of breathable air.

Humans. At first, J.C. thought perhaps YHWH's plan had worked, that he had stumbled back into a post-apocalyptic world where the mammals had quickly evolved to their most debauched and hedonistic, but the closer he looked, the more he was confused. There were few technological marvels here. In fact, a group of humans nearby had shed themselves of clothing entirely, and were dancing around in an almost religious fervor, buck naked. Two more were copulating on the ground, rolling around in each other's creamy filth, which had mixed with the mud to create a sort of human roux.

A long-haired man wearing strange rainbow-colored clothes, his hands raised to the sky, bumped into J.C. and hugged him.

"Sorry, brother! How you doin'? Everything groovy?"

"Are you worshipping?"

"Absolutely, brother. Feeling the vibes. Spiritual, you dig?"

These revelers didn't look familiar. Perhaps they were some obscure pagan sect worshipping Pikkiwoki, the Papua New Guinean mud god. "Did he promise you a pig and all the coconuts you can carry?" That was his usual M.O. He was fun at parties.

"You're a trip, man!"

A roaring buzz rang out over the field of bodies, and the crowd cheered. J.C. turned and there, in the distance, a huge stage had been set up. People with odd instruments were appearing on the stage under a cloud of acrid, blue smoke. A bizarre spectacle, indeed. "Wait, what year is it and where am I?" J.C. asked his new "friend."

Michael Allen Rose

"It's 1969 and you're in the middle of Max Yasgur's 600-acre dairy farm in Bethel, New York. Tune in, turn on, drop out, brother man."

A man with a similar complexion to J.C. himself was on the stage now, and began playing his stringed instrument. It was an instrumental version of "The Star-Spangled Banner", which J.C. remembered because the ghost of Francis Scott Key wouldn't shut the fuck up about it, humming it all over the afterlife. But in this version, the heavy sounds made J.C. smile from ear to ear. It took him a moment to recognize that he was looking at minor fire God, Jimi Hendrix.

"Far out," he said, patting this weird, dirty man beside him on the shoulder. There was a lot of love in this place. J.C. thought about the mammals that his father's forced evolution was creating. They might enjoy the debauchery, but they would never tap into the love.

J.C. meditated for a moment, allowing the music to wash over him. If he concentrated hard enough, he could actually see into other realities, and he tried to tune into the one that YHWH was trying to make. When he saw images of that reality, he was horrified. In that version of Woodstock 1969, nu metal had already been invented, and instead of a scorching Hendrix solo played for hippies fucking in the grass, a band that sounded exactly like Limp Bizkit was playing for a number of bros. "Everything would move so far up the timeline . . . these people won't have the necessary angst to handle nineties music in the sixties! I have to help them." J.C. fitted his goggles onto his face and blasted off for parts unknown, thinking about the meat-eor hitting the planet and the catastrophe that awaited them all if he failed.

All the thinking he was doing about Earth and space had the unfortunate effect of depositing him on a very Earth-like planet called Kepler-78b. Astronomers on Earth had once called this lava world an abomination. They thought that there was no physical way a small world, only twenty percent larger than Earth, could have evolved in that location and that there was no known mechanism that could have transported it there. They believed that it couldn't possibly roast in that hellish orbit for long and that it was destined to get swallowed by its star in the next three billion years or so.

He would have liked to tell them that, actually, the god Mercury had placed Kepler-

78b there as a place to put his keys, because he would often lose them, and he wanted something that reminded him of Earth, of which he was a fan. But that revelation was for another time.

This time, J.C. honed in on the things that made him Jesus, thinking about his life and adventures. This seemed like a better trail to follow than planetary themes, which were just shooting him around the galaxy at random. Perhaps his own breadcrumbs, left by a life of miracles, would help him find the place he'd left off.

He exited the strange planet in a burst of holy light, and when he arrived in his new location, he quickly felt the vibrations to see if he was anywhere close to his target. He was on Earth: check. He was in the Middle Eastern part of the planet: check. He was in a time before his second coming: check. This place felt very familiar. Had he finally done it? He opened his eyes.

He was in a strange bedroom, with bronze fixtures. Through the round porticoes in the walls, stood three immense and impressive towers. The walls were constructed with large, white marble stones, so exactly united to one another, that each tower looked like one entire rock in and of itself. He could see that each had large bed-chambers, containing beds for a hundred guests each. The roofs featured splendid ornaments. The room he was currently in featured furniture of silver and gold.

Outside, several groves of trees grew below, with deep canals, and cisterns In several places, brazen statues shot steady flowing streams of liquid. Dove-courts filled with tame pigeons and many more statues of precious metals dotted the landscape. Whoever lived here was rich, and definitely of a class near the top of the heap.

A door opened from a staircase below the room, and a bearded Roman walked in, whistling. He stopped short when he saw J.C., eyes wide. "Who in the hell are you and what are you doing in my bed chamber?"

It was King Herod the Great. J.C. smiled and cracked his knuckles.

Book 22

"**H**e broke my nose! Capture the intruder!"

Herod was laying at the bottom of a flight of stairs, bleeding and bruised. He was trying to yell commands to his guards, but his lip was so swollen and fat he didn't really sound like himself, so help was slow in coming.

"That's what thou gets for massacring innocent babies, thou sack of donkey semen." J.C. leaped from the window and landed like a ninja cat in one of the gardens.

"Hey does that guy look Jewish to y—?" one of the guards asked the guard next to him, just before J.C. grabbed both of their helmets and cracked them together. The sound was that of two coconuts smashed together between shields, and the men fell to the ground, unconscious.

"I could get used to this action hero stuff," J.C. said to himself, as he spun around to check his six. Up in the window, the broken and battered Herod had pulled himself up, and was now ranting about teleporting kings and how the prophecies were coming true. Jesus scowled and thumbed his nose at the shitty king. Herod was a dick. This was a man so concerned that no one would mourn his death, he gave an order that a large group of distinguished men should be killed at the time of his own death so that the displays of grief that he craved would take place. He had a little power to spare, and this guy deserved a little holy wrath. "Hey, thou ass! Catch this!"

J.C. summoned some of his power and sneezed a holy sneeze, sending celestial bits of magical mucus skyward. Like a fart loaded into an Airzooka, the packet of microbes flew straight and true, right into the face of the king. He gasped and choked, angrily flapping his arms. They would historically call this excruciatingly painful, putrefying illness of uncertain cause, "Herod's Evil," which is what ultimately killed him. J.C. considered making a quick pit stop and giving the same viral load to Adolph Hitler, but he was already afraid of having any further effect on the divergent timelines. Ultimately, he decided that at least humiliating such a horrible man would be appropriate, so he gave him one testicle, a stupid haircut, and made him a terrible painter. Similarly, he also ended up making one stop in the early twenty-first century to give a certain president tiny hands, maximum level dementia, and a miniscule penis, but that's a story for another time.

J.C. was bouncing around in history with reckless abandon, trying to find the right channel, but there were too many variables. He tried thinking about his old friends, the disciples and their adventures together. He tried concentrating on the void that might be left by the dinosaurs' disappearance. He tried thinking about other deities, his father included. It was exhausting, and confusing. By the time he stopped to rest, he had been to the sets of several Cecil B. DeMille movies including *King of Kings* and *The Ten Commandments*, Mount Olympus in Greece, the wastes of Siberia, and a cult compound in Texas, in the twentieth century United States.

Jurassichrist

Finally, after dozens of quantum leaps, J.C. ended up floating in space. In the wrong plane of Earth's trajectory after failing to account for not only the orbit of the sun, but the expansion of the universe. Space and time work in tandem, and he was tight with neither universal concept anymore. It was at this point that he finally admitted to himself that he was considering giving up. He floated there, among the stars, wondering why he was even trying anymore. It was probably too late. YHWH was all powerful, and with the constant use of his power, he was drained. The black cross was even starting to feel like it was running low on juice, and needed a recharge.

He floated in the black void, watching galaxies spiral and feeling sorry for himself.

Lost and alone, he drifted through space, letting time slip away in the darkness. He talked to himself for a little while, but there was no air to carry the sound waves, so it didn't do much to alleviate his loneliness. It just made his mouth kind of cold.

He floated through a cloud of interstellar gas, a beautiful orange haze that reminded him of sunsets on Earth. Space here was a bit more dense, and smelled strange, like a copper coin lathered up with grapeseed oil and stuffed up the nostril. The air here was just dense enough for vibrations to travel through it, and a few atoms per second could finally impact J.C.'s ultra-sensitive eardrum, which is the only reason he heard it:

"Hey. Hello. Hey, you."

Someone was speaking to him, here, in the deepest reaches of space. Might it be telekinetic, or it might be a fellow deity or traveler from another plane? The ice crystals that had formed on his face and head broke off and floated freely away as he twisted his neck to look around. The swirling gas rippled around him, but he saw no other lifeforms or celestial beings anywhere.

"Loki? Is that you? Art thou invisible again?"

There was no answer for a moment. Then, finally, a small voice, very much inside his head. "I am not a Loki."

"Ack!" The voice was so close, so invasive, he reflexively poked into his ear with his pinky finger and squeegied it around, wondering if he had a ball of loose wax bouncing around and irritating his eardrum.

"Please stop that. Your appendage is very big."

Jurassichrist

"Okay. Who's speaking?"

"Hello. I am Tardigrade. It is pleasant to see you again."

The familiar voice finally registered. "Tardigrade! How is it that you have come to this place? Wait . . . where art thou?"

"In your ear, god man rock fire creature that is nice. I remember you."

"You really are that tardigrade? What happened? How didst thou get to space?"

"Not sure. I remember eating some moss, and I think someone took the moss and took me and we went to a place where creatures that looked like you were moving things around, and they put me in a big tube and it shook and fire came out of its butt, and then I was on a floating station up here with a bunch of creatures that looked like you who wore white skins and little clear eyeball covers, and they talked about smart things in this place, and then one day the place exploded when a giant rock made of meat hit it and I flew this way, so now I'm just enjoying some vacation time."

"How didst thou survive? And why art thou awake now?"

"I did my cryptobiosis thing and became a tun. It was nice. Like a nap. Your ear moisture has awakened me. Thank you for your dampness."

"Thou art quite the survivor." J.C. used his celestially-enhanced sight to look omnisciently beyond the normal veil of space, and about a quarter of a light year away, there was a clump of floating debris and dead astronauts. "By my calculations, thou hast been around for approximately sixty-five million years."

"It was a long nap. No wonder I'm not sleepy." The tiny creature yawned adorably, wiggling its little arms above its head. "I recognized your scent. What are you doing here? I thought you spent your time in volcanoes?"

"I cannot find my way back there," said J.C. "I wish I could."

"How do you travel? Do you swim, too?"

J.C. felt the little creature tickle his eardrum. "No, I . . . how to explain . . . I have to think very hard about where I want to be, the time and the place, and then I have a power I use to get there."

"So, what is the problem?"

"I can't seem to find the key to getting back there again. Everything I try ends up taking me down a divergent path."

Jurassichrist

"Well, if you have to think about what is most important, maybe you should think about your friends. That's how I knew you. I thought 'Hey, that's my friend, the lava man who became calcium and gave me water to wake up.' Then I came over here."

J.C. wanted to high five the little creature, but he didn't want to squish anyone, and ultimately he'd just be slapping himself in the ear, so he settled for a warm, glowing smile. "I'll take your advice, little one."

"Great. You should never give up, strange creature. Look at me. I'm a Tardigrade!"

J.C. had never been so delighted to have used his powers to grant a living thing extra life. Lazarus was a close second, but this little guy was the best. It was comforting to know that whether he succeeded or failed, tardigrades would survive. Them, and cockroaches, anyway.

He thought about how he had landed in the time of the dinosaurs like a predator, blowing away anything unfamiliar, and how he had learned of the conspiracy against them. How he had come to find out about his father's true intentions, and how humans had been set up to take the fall by a mad god. He honed in on the dinosaurs once more, the way that Myron had treated him with kindness, even though he was not unlike a grizzly bear that ravaged a human campsite. The mammals would have murdered him in similar circumstances, and if YHWH had his way, they would be irredeemable, going down an evil path to become even more dangerous and deceptive, wallowing in their depravity.

He had jumped through the four most popular dimensions so many times that his senses were addled. Even his fnorkblart was off, making the other dimensions a bit off. It is impossible to describe what that is like to mortals, who sadly lack the sense fnorkblart, but the best description ever was probably from the Goddess Isis who had come up with it while making a golden penis replacement for Osiris and experimented by messing about with the fourth dimension and some cats. She said it was akin to tasting the color purple while feeling the sky and looking at the sound of a monkey screeching while listening to the concept of sleeping. (A side note: after a particularly bold attempt at time and space manipulation by Isis, one of those cats later appeared in the twentieth century laboratory of Erwin Schrödinger.)

Jurassichrist

He thought about all the creatures that needed his help. He pictured them, very carefully, tracing their features in his mind like an artist trying to capture the perfect life drawing. He remembered his fear upon seeing the monsters at first, and how he had learned about their true nature. Their mastery of magical metals. The hum. He actually began to hum himself, firstly trying to imitate it, and then, failing that, just letting his mind wander while humming a tune.

"Hmmmm hmmmm . . . from Kether to Malkuth. Ride your ass like a demon from station to station . . . "

He hummed harder, and although space didn't allow the sound to go anywhere, the vibrations were pleasant in his throat.

"That's nice. Soothing." The Tardigrade was apparently still in his ear.

"I almost forgot thee," J.C. said. "Wouldst thou like to go back to Earth?"

"Is there moss there?"

"Yes."

"Then, yes, I think I would."

J.C. concentrated his power to create a little bubble of water. He manifested some lichen and bits of plant matter inside it. In the zero-gravity environment, the water droplet stayed together, shimmering and wobbling. He placed it up to his ear. "Do you see the water?"

"I do!"

"Swim into it."

As the tardigrade swam, he spoke once more. "Thank you! See you later!"

J.C. doubted it, but then he wouldn't have expected to encounter the little critter again after the first time they had met. He placed a shield of holy protection around the water droplet to safeguard it on its path through the atmosphere, then he held it up and blew a mighty breath of Jesus magic, sending the droplet on a journey through space toward the planet Earth. Now, it was time for his own journey. He closed his eyes and thought about Myron's bone ridge, about the General's giant teeth, about the elderly Eoraptor, even about the shin wounds he'd suffered at the jaws of Officer Spingle.

Focusing all the power in the black cross, he opened a singularity around himself, and felt his very structure tear apart at the atomic level as the event horizon dawned. He felt his matter growing hot, and a glowing savior exploded into a powerful burst of cosmic radiation, blasting through the walls between dimensions and careening toward destiny.

J.C. opened his eyes to a vast red sky. He had done it. The volcano was in front of him, and even now it was smoking, threatening to erupt and consume the land surrounding it. The golden city was visible in the distance. He had landed almost exactly where he had started his second coming. "Well . . . twentieth coming or so is a charm," he muttered.

Everywhere, animals of all sorts were running and screaming, roaring and screeching with sheer terror. The Earth trembled and quaked. With his celestial hearing, he faintly heard the trumpets of Armageddon on the wind. The sun was red like blood. It was Revelations, only not just the written dreams of a crazy old man on an island: this was actually happening. No metaphors, just images of destruction, straight off the airbrushed side of a van. All that was missing was a wizard shooting lightning from his fingers, battling a dragon. J.C. might have to fill in for that wizard, if this went the way he thought it might.

The sky was filled with lightning, and deeper beyond the storms were two terrifying visions. First, a giant ball of festering meat, slowly tumbled through the cosmos, on a collision course toward Earth. Even now, tiny bits of the meat-eor rained from the sky, splashing down and making bloody puddles. Most of them were cooked to well done by the atmospheric re-entry, but some chunks were large enough to crush a car, and those were making quite a mess. J.C. watched as one of the slower, smaller lizards, some kind of skink, was flattened by a massive piece of muscle tissue.

Beyond that, filling the heavens to their very edges, the face of God, a gibbering, burbling eldritch nightmare. He was laughing maniacally, watching the impending doom of his creation. J.C. looked upon the face of the apocalypse. He gritted his teeth. He tore off a thin strip of his robe and tied it into a headband around his forehead. He unstrapped the Crucifixer from his back, removing the black cross at the core—and, wielding it like an axe, he began to climb the mountain before him, ready to confront the maker of the universe.

It was time for a final showdown.

Book 23

"**F**ather!"

J.C. stood on the rim of the volcano, screaming into the blustery sky. The wind was whipping his robes and hair nearly hard enough to drag him into the caldera, a fate he had already experienced once and wasn't keen to try again.

"Father! Answer me! You must stop this madness!"

The beast in the sky, unfathomable, indescribable, turned an infinite number of eyes upon the king of kings.

The beast burbled in infernal tongues, languages long forgotten and buried in the layers of the multiverse. Listening to YHWH speak this eldritch tongue was a little bit like trying to speak with Dagon, only without the terribly fishy breath blowing in your face. The destroyer/God stared at the tiny version of himself that had become a man, the goodness that he had once possessed, refined into this mortal vessel. His voice boomed in between the ears of Jesus. "There is no escape! Don't make me destroy you. You do not yet realize your importance. You've only begun to discover your power! Join me, and I will complete your training! With our combined strength, we can bring order to the galaxy."

"I'll never join you!"

"If only you knew the power of the dark side."

"Dark side?"

"Jesus, I am your father."

"Yes, I know that."

The God thing blinked its many eyes. "Search your feelings; you know it to be true!"

"Yes, I already know it to be true. That is why I stand in opposition to thee. I am taking responsibility for stopping thy wave of destruction. These creatures deserve it not." J.C. shook his head. "Get thee behind me, Dad! And, stop trying to get me to join thee, thou clichéd monster-of-the-week jackass! Thou shalt inherit my fist!"

Blasts of universe-shifting power bolted back and forth, as both of the celestials attempted to exert their strength. God's massive cannonballs of fury slammed against J.C.'s laser-focused beams of holy light, causing ripples of energy that bent time and space to be unleashed in every direction. The universe itself was shredding like wheat.

The beast in the heavens reshaped itself as J.C. tried to catch his breath. "Vengeance is mine, I will repay, says the Lord!"

God's shifting body erupted in an explosion of tentacles, and as a mass, they reached into the sky. With a roar, the supreme deity unleashed a barrage of fireballs. J.C. ran for cover, leaping over the flames bursting all around him. He skidded to a stop behind a massive chunk of splintered stone. A fireball hit the other side of his cover and shattered the rock into bits, stunning J.C. with a wave of immense heat.

J.C. rolled aside just in time to avoid being crushed by one of God's massive tentacles. It left a huge, smoking divot in the side of the mountain's peak. J.C. came up from the ground in a crouch and concentrated. A holy light emerged from the holes in his hands, and with a yell, he fired beams of yellow light into the sky. The monster who was YHWH didn't seem to notice, and two more tentacles crashed into the ground, causing a massive quake.

God manifested a gigantic hand, and brought the destructive power of the finger of God to bear on his only son. The fingertip began to glow white hot.

J.C. folded his arms in defiance. "Father, thou knowest that I am part of thine own holy trinity."

"So?" the voice boomed.

"So stop trying to finger thyself!"

YHWH pressed down, crushing a valley into the side of the mountain. Dust arose in plumes all around. After a few moments, holy light burst from beneath the fingertip, and J.C. appeared, lifting the digit off and hurling it back toward the heavens. The universe shuddered as God stumbled.

Battered, bloody, and bruised, J.C. stared down the creator of the universe. He fell to his knees, exhausted. Gritting his teeth, J.C. took his own finger and drew characters into the soil. "TERRA TERRAM ACCUSAT."

God laughed, a thunderous sound that knocked passing birds from the sky for miles around. "My old quip? Why bring up that chestnut? Times have changed, kiddo. I'm different. You're different."

"Earth accuses Earth. A mortal judges a mortal, a sinner accuses sinner. Thou art not greater than I, thou coked up freakshow. You are no master of creation, but a slave to your own selfish vices. I will not stop."

The cross had fallen from his back, the straps and mechanisms holding the Crucifixer to his slender body shredded and broken. A sharp pain in his shoulder told him it was dislocated. Gritting his teeth, he grabbed one arm with the other and shoved it backward, popping it into place with a huge crack. He stooped, and picked up the black cross, now pulsing with holy energy. It had been absorbing much of the energy used in the battle, and was hot to the touch. He struggled to right it, swaying and dizzy from the conflict.

"Then, you will die," the eldritch thing rumbled. "You should have listened to me. If you will not stop, I will stop you. And from this end, there will be no return. You've been to hell, you've been to the planes of death, but this time I shall cast you into oblivion, your matter vaporized and your consciousness sucked back into the deepest recesses of my omnipresence. You're too late to stop it, and you have failed."

The meat-eor now blocked out all the light in the sky, hurtling ever closer. It was heading straight for the impact zone, at which J.C. stood as a useful bullseye. J.C.'s super powers were many, but he could do little in the face of YHWH's omnipotent onslaught. He could frighten demons out of people, multiply food, transmute liquids into booze, hover, and even raise the recently dead, but he really was a healer, not a combat wizard. He couldn't freeze things with ice beams or turn anyone into a toad.

J.C. squeezed the huge cross in his hands. Its surface blazed with glowing, fiery red cracks. He knew that his own powers, though formidable, paled in comparison to his father's. The only way to beat him was to turn his own might against him, and there was currently only one thing holding the power of the lord outside the creature's physical form.

With a mighty grunt, J.C. lifted the cross upon his shoulders, feeling the heft. He whispered holy writ into the artifact: "Thou art my battle axe and weapon of war: for with thee will I destroy kingdoms." This was going to take absolutely perfect, pinpoint timing.

Jurassichrist

J.C. channeled his rage. He thought about all the humans to come, how their destiny was planted with poisoned seeds and how they reaped the horrible fruits of their ancestors fascinations. He thought about the dinosaurs, caught in the eye of his own monstrous father, brought to the edge of apocalypse due to a cosmic jerk who was jealous of their good nature and peaceful ways. He thought of his own ethereal brethren, conned into playing the part of the unwitting villains in this cosmic morality play. He swung for the fences, and the hit connected.

The impact was like a small thermonuclear explosion. The force wave blew J.C.'s hair back. If he hadn't been at the epicenter of the blast, he would have flown miles over the horizon and landed in a tar pit somewhere, but his holy magic held him fast. The meat-eor flew up, up, up, seeming to shrink as it hurtled toward the eye of YHWH himself.

The supreme being had not expected this turn of events, and was thusly unprepared to defend himself with the gargantuan missile slammed into the center of his pupil, burying itself for a moment in the unknowable skull of the divine. For a brief nanosecond, a stillness overtook the universe, as God's face showed surprise and horror for the very first time. Then, like a hollow point bullet, the meat-eor burst from the back of God's head, shattering reality and sending debris big-banging into the multiverse. The explosion was like nothing since the original beginning of time, with energy and matter expanding in fractions of a second, and then suddenly, the wave passed by.

God was dead.

Not in a Nietzsche kind of metaphorical way, but like, really, truly, dead. His corpse was as big as the universe itself, having been scattered into what amounted to yet another Big Bang, and everything from the smallest blade of grass to the largest red giant in some distant galaxy was beginning to change.

Yes, God was dead, but his remains would fertilize the universe.

Revelation

Michael Allen Rose

Heaven was very, very quiet. It hadn't taken long for the evidence to mount, after the Voice allowed other deities to investigate the office of God, and so the mortal realm was left in some degree of disarray. It was embarrassing, nobody having had any idea about the cosmic conspiracy. Athena questioned her own wisdom. Anubus folded his ears in shame. Various angels bumped into each other, flying idly around, wondering where it had all gone wrong. The only thing that they all agreed on: Jesus had saved the multiverse, and should not be held responsible for his patricide.

When the divine had been destroyed, all of his anachronisms had disintegrated along with him. Stripped of their ill-gotten As Seen On TV products, the mammals reverted to the level of development appropriate to their timeline. But that wasn't the only mess left that needed cleaning up.

It was said that the meek shall inherit the Earth. But, actually, J.C. inherited it. And he didn't want it.

J.C. had been sitting in his father's former office for days, sulking, thinking, reminiscing. He wondered if he could have done anything different. Whether his actions were ultimately for the greater good, or just a different sort of evil. Morality was already a gray area for most chronospatially challenged beings, but in this case, the ultimate arbiter of the very concept of morality had been exploded, so it was hard to figure out what kind of yardstick such things could be measured against.

He had spent what felt like eons making sure all the gears were turning and all the right buttons were pressed, just to ensure that the universe kept working while management was in flux. He had personally seen to the repair of over a hundred thousand rips in the fabric of space-time. He'd even picked out the color himself, which had led to a quantum realm covered in four-dimensional dots of chrono-resistant hyperblack, like a quickly patched apartment wall bespeckled with toothpaste. The dinosaurs had avoided their extinction event—well, one of them—and J.C. decided to leave well enough alone. Let them stick around and evolve. Maybe they'd become the new apex predator in a couple million years. Maybe they'd teach the mammals how to be better. Maybe they'd invent a better Detroit. This whole "creation" experiment hadn't worked with too heavy a hand on the wheel, so maybe the whole thing would be better off without the hand of the divine steering into a ditch.

He had worked his holy ass off, and although things were stable, the wide-open void of the unknown was both fascinating and terrifying before him. His father had always claimed to be omniscient. J.C. had proven that to be bullshit when he socked YHWH in the eye with his most powerful weapon. Still, J.C. was glad that omniscience didn't exist. He couldn't fathom what it might be like to actually live with a curse like that, which presented itself as a blessing.

At least, now that the rules were no longer writ in stone, so to speak, he didn't have to get nailed to anything to traverse the realms.

Michael Allen Rose

It was time for a little vacation.

J.C. sat, watching the rings of Saturn peacefully dance around their celestial orbit. He called up one of his oldest friends, with whom he butted heads sometimes, and things got fucked up between them occasionally, but with whom the shared history between them was too important to allow their connection to wither.

"They're pretty, my Lord."

"Thanks. They were my idea. Father thought them too gaudy, but I told him if thou lovest something, thou ought to put a ring on it. It's one of my favorite planets."

J.C. glanced over when his companion cleared his throat. The human looked so fragile. In a way, J.C. envied that. So much power was difficult to bear.

"So, what wilt thou do? Wilt thou ascend to thine father's throne?"

J.C. pondered for only a moment, then shook his head. "No. I've seen enough of what happens when gods toy with mortals, first hand. The policies that we enact, they harm people, change them, make their lives difficult and strange. I've got a few billion years worth of examples. No, they don't need God. They need to find their own way, and roll with whatever happens."

"Maybe they'll even learn to take care of each other." The two friends sat in silence, soaking in their own heavy thoughts.

"I'm giving up my Godhood." J.C. snapped, and a massive thunder peal shook the foundation of heaven.

"What didst thou just do?"

"I'm going back, but not as a deity. I'm going to get born again. Learn to walk. See the sights. Drink a few beers with friends. Try to make the world a better place from the bottom up. I don't think you can define what it is to be human unless you really become one. Last time was a hoot, but I was still throwing miracles around like they were going out of style. This time, straight-up mortal. No tricks. I'm just going to do the best I can."

"What of death?"

"I'm not sure yet. I've kind of done that already, and it's not great. I think I might just keep my head down, blogeth about what goes on, try to help in smaller ways."

"Hmmm. No death. No divine guidance. That's new. And, what if someone notices the power vacuum and steps in to try their hand?"

J.C. chuckled, raising an eyebrow. "Why? Art thou thinking of selling me out again for thirty pieces of silver?"

"Ach! The thirty pieces of silver thing again! Art thou ever going to let me forget that?"

"No dude, you got me crucified!"

"It was part of thy father's plan! Thy father, who art a total dick, and who hadst ulterior motives from the beginning, as thou hast revealed to me!"

J.C. pondered. "That's true, actually. You have a point, old friend."

Judas Iscariot clapped his bestie on the shoulder. "So, if this be so, what happens to me? And, what happens to the rest of us? Those of us long dead and in the prime of our afterlives?"

"Everything pretty much stays the same for the moment. Until we figure out what to do. The heavens are basically a bureaucracy. Dost thou really think the Voice of God will just go home? They are a workaholic!"

"A what?"

"It's an Earth word. Don't worry about it. But still, just because the CEO gets fired doesn't mean the company shuts down and the workers stop doing what they do."

"Your time travels have made your words

bizarre. I do not envy the future. So, we are to just go about business as usual? Without any deities running things?"

J.C. nodded at the planet before them. "I could speak to Saturn. He's fun at parties."

"Doesn't he devour his children?"

"Only some of them." J.C. shrugged. "But I don't know, I think humanity will be all right. They either learn to swim, or they sink."

"That's a lot of faith you're putting in humanity, Lord."

Jesus of Nazareth, soon to be Jesus of somewhere like Cleveland or Paris or Dinotopia or Buenos Sauros, stared into the middle distance, the corners of his mouth turning downward. "It's about time they had to feel the burden of having faith put in you. I've had to deal with it for millennia. Let's find out what happens when they have to learn to get along."

Saturn cast her shadow upon the rings, which kept implacably floating there, like a halo, regardless of light or darkness, just as they had since creation.

Amen

About the Author

Michael Allen Rose is a writer, musician, editor and performance artist based in Chicago, Illinois. His stories have appeared in *The Magazine of Bizarro Fiction*, *Heavy Feather Review*, and *Tales From The Crust* among other periodicals. He has published several books including *Embry: Hard Boiled* (Eraserhead Press), *Rock And Roll Death Patrol* (Rooster Republic Press), *The Indifference Of Heaven* (Omnium Gatherum) and more. He is the host of the annual Ultimate Bizarro Showdown at Bizarro Con in Portland, OR. Michael also releases industrial music under the name Flood Damage and writes for the online surrealist magazine *Babou 691* as creator of the regular feature "Arcade Anomalies". He lives with an awesome cat, helps his girlfriend make internet porn, and enjoys good tea.

The Perpetual Motion Machine Catalog

Antioch | Jessica Leonard | Novel

Baby Powder and Other Terrifying Substances | John C. Foster | Story Collection

Bleed | Various Authors | Anthology

Bone Saw | Patrick Lacey | Novel

Born in Blood Vol. 1 | George Daniel Lea | Story Collection

Crabtown, USA:Essays & Observations | Rafael Alvarez | Essays

Dead Men | John Foster | Novel

Destroying the Tangible Issue of Reality; or, Searching for Andy Kaufmann | T. Fox Dunham | Novel

The Detained | Kristopher Triana | Novella

Gods on the Lam | Christopher David Rosales | Novel

Gory Hole | Craig Wallwork | Story Collection

The Green Kangaroos | Jessica McHugh | Novel

Invasion of the Weirdos | Andrew Hilbert | Novel

Last Dance in Phoenix | Kurt Reichenbaugh | Novel

PERPETUAL MOTION MACHINE PUBLISHING

Patreon:
www.patreon.com/pmmpublishing

Website:
www.PerpetualPublishing.com

Facebook:
www.facebook.com/PerpetualPublishing

Twitter:
@PMMPublishing

Newsletter:
www.PMMPNews.com

Email Us:
Contact@PerpetualPublishing.com

Printed in the USA
CPSIA information can be obtained
at www.ICGtesting.com
LVHW031346171023
761319LV00010B/1061